[T-]

Kevin [signature]

By Kevin Anthony Kautzman

For Bob and Genny,
in gnosis.

Thanks:

peggytoddmonicaemanuelsharlowbettykellenchelseyfuzz
danslaterjulesjasonfeserjasonkrausericdanmeidingerjoe.o
joe.gjoe.oalsenseijonshawnalikatenolanrobbrandonbran
donbrandonjessicaaaronmattnickristeneidetollefsonlarat
heborealisthebookhouseevanmarkmichellelevilevitwinciti
esaikidocentermegsethpetersonjustino'brienjimlisaandfa
milylangeskautzmanshansonallthemusiciansandartistsallt
helightbearersallthethinkersandanybodyelsewhohurtorhe
lpedorbothandbeyond

IT-I was written over ten days in July of 2002. It was originally published – a chapter each day – through an online journal and has since been removed. The following is an edited version of the piece, with the original work mostly intact. No content has been changed.

a·poc·a·lypse

Apocalypse *Abbr.* Apoc. *Bible.* The Book of Revelation.

1. Any of a number of anonymous Jewish or Christian texts from around the second century B.C. to the second century A.D. containing prophetic or symbolic visions, especially of the imminent destruction of the world and the salvation of the righteous.

2. Great or total devastation; doom: *the apocalypse of nuclear war.*

3. A prophetic disclosure; a revelation.

[Middle English Apocalipse, from Late Latin Apocalypsis, from Greek apokalupsis, *revelation, Apocalypse,* from apokaluptein, *to uncover* : apo-, *apo-* + kaluptein, *to cover*; see kel-[1] in Indo-European Roots.]

From www.dictionary.com.

I say the end is near...

Æternus in Ten Steps

10 Days

6:10 P.M.

The world is going to end in ten days, and what follows will be my record, the recording of my experience of the spacious, *infinite* macrocosm's conclusion. Here, for you, is a message of the end, from the end of an era, from the end of all eras, for you to wallow around in, contemplate, loathe, and, if you intend to take this prophecy seriously, fear.

Do I need to say that we fear the unknown? If you don't know that, then you're stranger than you look, sound, smell. I'll say it then. *We fear the unknown.* And when most everybody doubts if we can know anything, that amounts to a whole lot of fear.

As for the end of the universe – that's a big *if*, isn't it? A big unknown, and thus also a big fear. Here's some of what I *know*.

Every phone number, credit card number, social security number, password, key-code, alphanumeric record you've ever made it a point to remember will be irrelevant. There aren't going to be any phones, any banks, any stores, or any government – because there won't be anything at all – in ten days from this moment, or, I should say, the moment that I started writing this journal. I hope you're a fast reader, for your sake.

I've known that the world is going to end ten days from now for about a day. This means that, when

I discovered that the end was nigh, the game's near up, the fat lady's about to sing, I had eleven days in which to decide what to do about it. Now I have ten days. If you're reading this journal and it's, say, the 17th, then you have ten days minus T to prepare yourself for the end of the world. T in this equation is however long it has taken for you to receive and start reading this journal. Maybe you have only *minutes*.

I don't want to start a panic. The individual condition is too precarious for most. I wouldn't want anybody to waste their last days doing anything ridiculous. It wouldn't surprise me if the television networks know the truth but aren't saying anything. There are some smart people behind the television. I don't mean the actors or anybody who actually works on the shows. I mean the people behind the television.

Anyway, whatever plots and plans exist for the future order of the world and the continued conditioning of its people won't matter much in nine days, twenty three hours, and forty six minutes. That's just under two hundred and forty hours. That's fourteen thousand three hundred and eighty six minutes. That's about 863,160 seconds – less, really, because it's taken me time to calculate this, write it down, and for you to read it.

Maybe I should tell you more about myself. You

wouldn't want to trust just anybody with this kind of news. But if I tell you more about myself, you'll only have more areas to project your disbelief upon. Ultimately, it's irrelevant. Belief is such a thin front. Mostly it's about self-confidence. You can only really believe in yourself, or... I can only really believe in myself, ultimately. But we're all a part of a larger sphere, I speculate, and maybe that's what I mean by "the world." I just know that I was given a message yesterday in such a way that it must be true.

If you're reading this, you have some serious thinking to do, because if you're reading this you must be reading it somewhere between when I started and when the world's going to end. Nobody's going to read what I say after the world's over, because nobody will be reading. There won't be any world: no home computers, no annoying foreign languages you can't understand, no gas stations, no "Virgil" the manager of E-Z Crunch Gas Emporium, and definitely no you or me. So who can read what's not there? Consciousness requires an object and a subject, last I checked, and when the world ends, earth alone isn't going to explode like in some ridiculous, formulaic Hollywood psychic-nightmare trap. No. I mean the macrocosm itself: the whole thing. The great gracious span. Boom, click, pop, slish, slosh – and gone. I suspect it will make all those sounds and more, because for all this to end, the infinite paradox must occur. All things will cease. What kind of a sound does that make? I guess we'll find out.

There's a police car outside the gas station where I work. I think about going outside to see what's happening. It will get my mind off the terrible truth I know. It's difficult to take people's credit cards to ring up their gas when I know the whole economic system's not just going to crash but will, in less than ten days, completely blip out of existence.

I can only make out the police car's lights on top, which aren't on, and the car's ass end. I'm sure it has something to do with the bum-fuck kids who beg for change. One of them fell asleep on the sidewalk earlier, and a whole gang of firemen showed up for some reason. I don't know who would call the police because there's a bum sleeping on the ground. Maybe they thought he was dead.

I go outside, and yes, I was right. The cops, a large, tall man, and a very masculine-looking women are confronting three grungy, smelly, street-kids. The kids have a dog, which lies on the pavement and pants – it doesn't even seem bothered. I think it's very funny – if they knew what I know, maybe the roles would be reversed. Maybe the kids have always lived as if the world's going to end, and maybe the cops have always been sandbagging against an impossible flood – a good image. And then there's the dog.

The dog is large and black and has deep brown eyes. It glances my way as the cops get into their cruiser. One of the kids stands up, dirt caked over his thick tan. He looks ugly and frail, uncomfortable in all moments: street *stupid*. His shirt says: "Starfucks, Fuck Off. Get the fuck out of my neighborhood."

His neighborhood? Clearly the cops differ on that point. The kids seem pleased that they aren't being arrested, a small territorial contest they think they've won. But anyway, the kid in the Starfucks shirt knows as well as the rest of us that it's not "his" neighborhood. The neighborhood belongs to the strips of businesses and the well-dressed people with cel-phones. The neighborhood belongs to people like Virgil.

Virgil is inside when I get back. He does not look pleased. He never looks pleased. Virgil looks like a decrepit, older versions of one of the street kids. Combine the Starfucks kid with the female cop and you'd have a more attractive version of Virgil, maybe one of his cousins – this man is my boss. In the economic system of twenty-first century America, there is one rule: pricks rule. Virgil is not an exception to this rule. Not that it matters.

[T-] 8

"So'in mer in'eres'ing 'an yer joooab?"

"Just some kids outside, the cops and all."

"Shawr. T'os li'el shoits aw' alwis bummin' smokes 'an buggin' cus'mers," Virgil slurs. He pauses, as if deep in thought. I doubt if the man's capable of the most elementary logic. I can imagine what that would sound like:

"Virgil -- truly though art named well, for thine words are shining jewels and your voice rings, resonates in mine ears like soft, tinkling bells – will you tell me? If A then B, and I supply a gracious A – what happens next? What follows that A? Multiple choice: A, B, C, or D."

"Mmm. 'das a tuffy."

"Shawr is Virgil. C'mon, though you can do it! Let me give you an example."

"'at'd be good."

"So... First let's set our variables: A is – you get smashed in the face with a nine-iron – and B is – Virgil starts to enunciate his words so that even the hard-of-hearing might have one chance in a million to understand him. So, if A, then B, what does that mean?"

"Means ay' gi' hi' wi' a nayun aye'run..."

"And..."

[T-] 9

"Ai'm na' shawr."

"Great. Well, perhaps we can move on to a more advanced topic, such as the paradoxical notion that some thing, say X, can both equal and not equal another thing, say Z. What do you think about that?"

Probably nothing. What can you say about the divine, infinite confusion, that superb dichotomy between... everything? Not a whole lot before you start to flap your lips and make silly noises.

I come out of my fantasy to see Virgil flipping through my magazine, part of the ineffable 'Muff-Divers' collection, loaned to me from – of all people – my girlfriend. And why not?

I pull the magazine away from his bony fingers and stare at him, first at his left eye, then his right, and finally at the bridge of his bubbly nose. He seems to be looking back at me, but I can't tell. His eyes are dead, like most the people who come into this cheesy little pointless hole in the wall gas-haven.

"Noice tit's 'ere. M.m.?"

I just nod my head and pretend to look at the magazine. I can't focus with this throwback stooping over me. He sounds as if he has golf balls for wisdom teeth, and right now I'd give anything for an iron. I won't miss him when the world ends. In fact, I find a mildly pleasant, tingling sensation when my regular hatred for this man twice my age – he's about forty, looks sixty – bubbles from my gut into my brain, the coiled snake of dark Kundalini kissing my personal ego-epicenter, that gorgeous little black space I hold so close. Why is this pleasant? Beyond the pure sex-appeal of the notion of complete annihilation, I've just realized that there's absolutely no reason for me to keep working at this Gas-Head's paradise.

No more credit cards. No more toilet paper gunk beneath my fingernails from cleaning up piss and vomit and semen. No more street kids asking me for change. No more gas-stench. And best of all, no more Virgil.

I studiously ignore Virgil's pathetic milling about for company as I return to my seat. Between where I sit and guard the cigarettes and the counter there stands an inch-thick layer of bullet-proof plexiglass, or whatever it's made out of. Once last year a very smart looking – that is, smart enough to wear a black ski mask – meth addict held the store up by gunpoint. I remember it was very hot that day – no clouds, middle of the summer. I was the only person in the building. That's the only time I've ever been glad about the glass between myself and the rest of the world. Every other moment at this job has felt impersonal, unreal – the hours piled upon one another in a meager excuse for human life.

My girlfriend – her name's Bea, and she doesn't know about all this yet. I mean, she doesn't know that the world's going to end – has always said I'm not motivated enough, that I'm intelligent enough to be somebody important if I'd only let myself be inspired. About the only motivation I do have – or... did have, before I found out that the world's going to end: now I don't have any motivation, really, except to write this, and even this is tenuous and strained, because what's the point? Would you mind if I stopped? Sorry. I'm sure you've already started to blame me for a lot of all the fucked up problems I'm sure you have. I've just recently given you what might be the worst news of your life: worse than your father's suicide or your parents divorce or your not-getting-into-that-nice-college. Maybe I've given you good news. "The Good News." The New Gospel. The Gospel according to The Messenger. It is a gospel of annihilation, not of redemption... of judgement without the satisfaction of a decision.

Where was I? About the only motivation I do have is to get out from behind this glass, but that would mean leaving this job, and until now I've only been able to handle the most mediocre position with the littlest amount of responsibility you can imagine. Now I don't see any reason to keep this job. Before rent's due again, the world's going to end, so you can forget about phone bills, car payments, and all your debts.

It's possible that what we're coming to is judgement day – the ultimate karmic bill, the complete association of all our past transgressions piled together in a single moment of absolute agony-torture-bliss ride. What's that going to be like? Pure consciousness or pure sleep: can you be stoic and see the face of the people you've scorned, teased, hurt, charmed, fucked, killed, loved, hated, scammed, broke, made, all climb up your right leg and start licking your thigh? And maybe stoicism's over-rated and we all need to scream and panic once in a while.

I eat a strawberry. Strawberries, contrary to a certain collective of nitwits who argue for the mango, are easily the sexiest fruit. Imagine a giant strawberry being lowered into a swirling, black-hole style melt of white chocolate, and that's how I describe good sex, particularly good sex with Bea. You want to talk about losing the microcosm to the macrocosm, the small to the large – well, if you know, you know. I'm going to miss the sex.

I think about how I'm going to quit this job. It's near twilight. Virgil's mumbled something and appears to be leaving. Aside from Virgil, the meth-heads, and the plexiglass divide, this place has been mostly tolerable. I've gotten to "read" all the porn I want and have been able to listen to my own music. Some nights I've been able to sleep through half the shift without a single customer bothering me. I sleep a lot. I wonder how I'll sleep in the coming week and a half. I wonder how you'll sleep. I hope I haven't ruined a honeymoon or a vacation you've planned. Anyway. Don't blame the messenger. Whatever baggage you have you brought on this flight with you. It's not my fault if you're going to have to toss it overboard.

I step out the back and get into my car. I start the engine and enjoy the kick of the music that blares from my speakers. If William Blake were alive today, he'd sing in a progressive metal band and confuse the hell out of the banal throngs that would flock unwittingly to his concerts.

"X equals Z. X does not equal Z. Both are equally true," I can hear Mr. Blake scream into the microphone on stage. "Tygrrrrr.... Tygrrrr...." He has a beautiful singing voice, and he understands what's happening beneath the words. He does a blistering duet with some short guy in a wig, and the crowd, recognizing the short man... completely intoxicated and hypnotized, goes wild.

The ladies go wild for William. T-Shirts are made and sold. Concerts sell out in record time, all for the once-almost-forgotten poet and painter.

I peel my car around the corner. The tires make a loud screeching noise. Virgil notices me from where he stands beneath the glaring gas-station lights. A brief flicker of recognition gives his eyes more flare than I've ever seen in them, and he blinks once or twice. He glances over his shoulder – I'm turning slowly as this happens – to see that, no, I'm definitely not at the counter. I turn and head out of sight before he has a chance to react further, and over the speakers the music comes crystal clear – I'm hearing things I've never heard before. With great knowledge comes great responsibility, and I only know one thing: the day the world will end.

I can't breath. I'm choking. It feels moist. I feel tense. I can feel sharp little hairs pricking against my face like pins. I'm in between worlds right now, in between moments. I can sense Bea. She's all around me. I feel subsumed, beneath her, warm and cold at the same time.

I feel complicated. Do you know that feeling? I don't mean to say that I have complicated feelings – I do, but that's not what I'm describing. *I* feel complicated. I feel like if you looked inside of me you'd see a plate of spaghetti, and illumination, nirvana, peace, is the plate... but you can't see the plate because the spaghetti's so thick and tangled. You could never eat it all in one sitting, and moving it off the plate is impossible because it's cold and the sauce is crusted over.

I feel complicated like that.

I have this theory. Most everybody's wearing bowling shoes. People don't want anybody to know that they're wearing those comfortable, garage-sale bowling shoes, so they make sure to have something cover them. They spend hours picking out a different pair of shoes, trying on pair after pair, picking and choosing, choosing and losing... just to have the right pair of shoes to cover the dopey bowling shoes underneath. Sometimes the shoes they wear over their real shoes are bulky and make them walk funny, like a pair of high heels that are impossible to master. They don't mind a little bit of a hobble in their walk, as long as everybody knows that they're wearing nice, clean, fashionable shoes.

A woman in a nice black dress walks down the catwalk.

"She's beautiful," Ross the cameraman says.

"She sho' is," Buck the pornographer says. Buck's the hardest brick in the proverbial wall. His eyes burn with the fire of somebody who never – not in a million years – expects to evolve beyond the earthly biped. And why should he? "Got fay-un tits, n', n', n'. I'd ride her."

The woman walks up the catwalk and smiles. From the neck down she looks as if she's ready to hump a pole. From the neck up she's a lifeless, sophisticated mess with dead eyes. It's clear she's not with the rest of them.

Fucking pigs, *she thinks. But she has the last laugh. The night is ruined when the men notice something terrible.*

"What's she wearing on her feet?" Ross the cameraman asks Vicki the designer. Vicki, red hair and sharp, menacing eyebrows, almost collapses.

"Aw' those bowlin' shoes?" Buck asks, snorting and

laughing. Guffaw ha ha.

The women in black turns around with a sharp toss of her head and walks back. She snorts some coke and later dies in a terrible car accident, but still – she got the last laugh. Even while flying through the windshield at ninety miles an hour, she still got the last, coke-crazed laugh. She is crushed beneath the piled wreckage of the car, and the police locate her by the bowling shoes that stick out from beneath the wreckage, the wicked witch of the east end.

Then there are people that can't put shoes on at all, not even a first pair. They can't wear shoes because they've got a terrible fungus between their third and fourth toes, or they've had their toes cut off by a torturous parent or sibling: it happens. For whatever reason, they can't wear the fashionable shoes that everybody else wears. These people tend to point out that everybody else really wears bowling shoes beneath their heels, and so they aren't very popular at parties.

And there are the people who don't *choose* to put shoes on at all – these are the folks that could wear them but, for whatever reason, opt against the social regularity and go for a more natural look. Some days I feel like one of those people. Everybody can see my wicked pasta on those days, and sometimes I feel like it works. Sometimes it's enough to show people your soul – your sole? Ho ho. But not usually. Usually you have to be careful about what you're wearing, because people *judge*. That's just what we do. How can we not?

My favorite people are the ones who paint their bowling shoes and make them into clown shoes: the laughers like that lady in black – in the vision – who got the last laugh, the people who know that the world's going to end, like me, but can't be sure when. At this point in my life – a very important point in the history of the entire macrocosm, surely, because it's all going to end very shortly, as you're already aware – I feel like I could paint everybody's shoes purple and get the great cosmic laugh, a final hiccup from the lawyers and the bankers and the students and the travelers and the musicians and even the clowns themselves. Ha ha ho ho: what matters? Who matters? What's matter? It's all gone, done, and the games up. Let's have a beer and play cards.

"We can't play cards without rules*," they'll shout at* me.

"To hell with it. Let's make a house out of them, and when the world ends, it might be the only thing left standing."

"Baby, give me a finger," I hear through Bea's

pink, moist, fleshy thighs-vagina-legs above me, crushing to my face and neck. "I'm almost there."

I can breath again, but only briefly. I open my eyes and take a good, long sniff of Bea's crotch, which she grinds – like the cosmic wheel of the ages – against my now-slippery face. Again and again she bobs herself against me, up and down my lips, so far up that I feel the nub of her clit jab against my nose, so far down that I inhale the strong scent of her ass as she moves. I don't bother holding her. My hands are at my sides, and I let her do as she pleases. I stick my tongue out between thrusts, jabbing it up as best and as deeply as I can. When I replace my tongue I'm rewarded with a moan. I live and die for that moan. More important that the cosmic Om is the cosmic groan.

"Oooooooohhhmmm........ mmmhhhoooooooO"

in – out – in – out – in – out – in – out

This is how the end will feel. You'll be on your back with something on top of you: something that you feel like you understand, but you really don't know a thing about. She's that thing, Bea – she's Z and I'm X in this

[T-] 21

equation. X both equals and does not equal Z... in the same moment and in all moments.

This is how the end will be. You'll be sticking your tongue into a cavern of honey, a bright pink, beautiful light, and then nothing. You'll be smothered in her folds. Time is essentially a masculine thing. It presses constantly onward, a stupid, mindless prick – like Virgil – fucking every one of us, forever. Art captures time and is accordingly feminine in nature: the yoni that swallows the lingam. When time ends, all concepts of separation will cease: femininity beyond the feminine. Concepts will disappear. The end of your life, the end of the universe, the end of every moment – everything is sex and not sex, X and Z, this and that. The difference here is that in nine days, we'll be down to two polar notions. Maybe they'll be reconciled. Maybe it won't matter.

Between the X and the Z there is always a victim, a giver and a taker. It might not seem like a reasonable assertion at the moment – I'm on my back, she's on top; she's mostly in control – but I've always thought of Bea as the victim between us. Surely it has something to do with my own insecurities: I've never been able to get over the feeling that all sex is an act of rape. It must not be, because we've been together for over a year, and the only solution to the compelling question – why we stay together? – involves a complicated system of projection, self-loathing, apathy, and sex-addiction. That's not to say that she and I don't love each other. Who the hell knows what that means, ultimately, so why not just use the word and go forward with all the socially acceptable tripe it brings?

"I love you," we sometimes mutter, our heads down, our necks twisting around, eyes darting frantically. Sometimes we can fake it. Sometimes we can fake it. Sometimes we can.

That seems to be what she and I do. Except, we don't really socialize with much of anybody reputable, so why we even bother deluding one another is beyond me. We all lie to ourselves because we're afraid that if we don't, other people will see the truth of what we are more clearly than we could ever see ourselves. You see, it's a wicked pattern – we lie to ourselves because we think it'll help us get along with other people, which is false, false, false, but we hate the idea that we alone have the answers that will solve the questions. Nobody outside of you will ever know you better than you know yourself. Bea and I lie to one another – and thus also to ourselves – I think, mostly for one another. But that might be a lie. The thing may be wholly selfish. It's a terrible thought, but calming. Honest.

We're a one way street, she and I. I don't know

where she thinks the street leads. I know where it leads, or at least I do now. A week ago I didn't have a clue, but now things are different. I *know* where the street goes, and it's literally a dead end – more than dead, far worse and even more *simple* than one simple word. It's not even an end. It's just... I can't imagine, but we'll find out, you and I, together, when it happens. The end of the world. The big un-bang. The big... nada, nil, nihil, finito, end-of-all-possibilities. This will happen to all of us, some day soon.

Back to the situation at hand, though. When I say I've always thought of Bea as a kind of victim, I mean it literally. Half the time I feel deranged. I'm aware that you project your own anxieties onto other people. People call that projection "psychology" or "the devil" or any other number of choice word-noises, to rationalize away the sheer terror of this situation in which we live. It's inevitably stronger, the projection, with people you love and see every day.

The person I see every day, regardless, is Bea, so she's the object of most my wild projectile dysfunction. We live together in a basement apartment just a few blocks away from the gas station, the one where I worked until seventeen hours ago... give or take. We've lived together since a week after we met last summer.

I remember meeting her at a show in a friend's

basement – The House of Knaves, a kind of flop-house turned bad-punk-rock-in-the-basement venue – during one of the more exciting keg-parties. We hit it off and rutted like rabbits that same night. We had a scare shortly after that. We thought she was pregnant. She wasn't. I don't know what we would have done if she had been.

A starship's captain in the distant future stands at the bridge of his vessel. He is surrounded by his weathered-crew, the victors in a thousand battles, the hunters and the hunted... famous for their resolve, their heroism, and their terrible dialogue.

"Aye' see aw' fetus, Cap'n! Five pa-ersec's awa-ey. Wha' wi' wa' dewwwww?!" the engineer asks him through his thick, cum stained beard.

The captain stares violently forward. "Prepare to abort fetus."

"Aye."

The crew stares in awe as it approaches what looks like a little lizard, its heart beating, beating, beating...

"Miss'els reaay', Cap'n."

A giant cigarette appears from the front of the ship. The heat from the fetus' heart sends light and warmth to the

cigarette. The captain shouts, "Fire!" and a giant lighter
appears, by which the cigarette is lighted. The captain wipes
some sweat from his brows.

"Aye' dinnae ken' if shae' cun tayke et', Cap'n."

The crew waits in anticipation as the captain orders,
"Launch carcinogen." The fetus dies in a puff of acrid
smoke. Mission accomplished. Stardate – every fucking day.

Bea, the child we never had – thank Buddha –
and I ended up living together in my apartment. She
had been between homes at the time, until she moved in
with me. I don't know much about where she comes
from. I've never met her parents, and she's never met
mine. That conversation had been brief.

"What'dyer' parents do?" she'd asked.

"I don't know. They used to kick the shit out of
me."

"Oh."

"What do yours do?"

"I don't want to talk about it," she'd said. Then
we lost ourselves between space, as we're so good at
doing.

If the fundamental building blocks of the

universe never touch each other and everything is relative, what does that say about the human condition? Not a lot, I think, if you're one of those people who think that most of our experience is governed by the outmoded Newtonian vision of physics... cause and effect and all that. If you're a person who has a more quantum outlook, it might say a lot to you. You decide, I guess. The quantum hologram's a fancy idea, but it doesn't explain a good blowjob.

Or does it?

I have a license to discuss the human condition because the world's nearly come to an end, and I'm the one who knows – as far as I can tell – and has openly declared the time and date. This gives me a PhD in end-of-the-worldology, simply out of necessity. I'm not suggesting that I was chosen... rather, that I *chose*. The distinction is important, isn't it? I wouldn't want to make this a mystical enterprise. I'm into hard, cold facts – yes, crippling and cold western-eyed outlook. Black and white, that's all I want to see, that's all I know we'll find. Here's life: black. Here's the end of life: white. It's that simple. Isn't it? Isn't that what most of us think? It's what I see around me.

The conclusion of my observations about myself and those around me is that we – this generation, all generations – are the neo-stoics, the in-betweeners, the kids of emptiness – aren't we? Aren't you? Who's not? Raise your hand and you get the stick. I'm the doctor here, and you're the undergraduate. Why? You don't believe me yet, that the world's going to end. You'll never get to graduate school because you'll never believe me, and when the world ends, it just ends, so you won't have time to change your mind. It's a Catch-22 – I think. Ask an English major.

Bea knows all about the distance between people. She works as a waitress at a bar in a fashionable area: poor and rich, X and Z. She talks about that sometimes, and we both agree that money is a terrible burden and we should just burn all the bills and melt all the change. We should go to a straight barter system, trading furs for food for beads for sex. You'd immediately see who's fucking who and who's on top, not this bullshit facade. Oh well. There won't be time for that, will there?

Bea's body? That's important, especially in a system of barter. She has a deep scar just beneath her left breast, but otherwise she's perfect: deep, delicious blond hair, cut short and sharp – sometimes ratty because she doesn't wash all that well – a nice body, firm, perky tits, and most importantly she's not afraid to play around. She's a tigress.

Since I've been with her the only other people

I've slept with, aside from Bea, have been the girls or guys she and I meet and bring home. It never lasts long – these are party people and travelers – but I enjoy myself, and Bea seems to have a good time for herself. She sometimes needs coaxing, but I never do. I'm always game for a toss, a go, a fuck, a menege' twaaaaaaahhh.

"What do you think about *her*, baby?" she'll ask. Her voice like corn coming off of the cob.

"She's nice," I'll slur. I'll be drunk on cheap local beer. "Nice ass."

"I like her eyes." She'll look distant now, half confused. I'll be smiling.

"Yeah. Let's go talk to her."

And we will. Go talk to her – that is. It happens whenever we needed something to do. I think she knows that without the wonderful possibilities of the three-ways I would have kicked her out long ago. I think that defines our relationship, more than any notion of love ever could. I like the feeling of new sex – the kind you get from somebody you've just recently touched. I need that. It wakes me up, keeps me keen and sharp. Anybody who denies that – who denies the desire for newness – is repressed. They're still covering their clown shoes.

Bea's sure not repressed. She's charming enough to be manipulative. She's waited tables for a long time, and that takes a certain kind of person. I've seen the way she deals with customers. She's got a bite to her. Her eyes get this twisted look, like they don't belong in her face. She gets that look when she tongues another women or when she gets it from one of our guy friends. She makes noises, not the moans she's making right now but strange noises, like she's not sure if she's in pain. I like that.

Sometimes people look like animals. Sometimes people look like *people*. More often, to me, people look like animals – so full of *need*. My favorite moments are the ones where people look like people, but those are rare. Don't you think?

"That man looks like a walrus."

Waitresses laugh, little chirps that will eventually, with age, grow into twisted, evil laughs, and eventually into full-fledged cackles.

"That one looks like a duck," they agree about

another one of the restaurant's customers.

Quack quack.

Hidden drinks behind the counter. Yum. The waiters and waitresses fall over one another in a great orgiastic heap. All flirting and flattery comes to an abrupt end. The customers watch in stunned awe as the rutting begins: pure, uninterrupted fucking. Get close to the source of food, and you'll see where the sex is. It's only a matter of time before even the most puritanical of the restaurant's patrons join in the wild, food-induced orgy of fluid exchange and sexual liveliness.

At the end of the night, the waiters and waitresses clean used condoms from the tables along with their – now larger than usual – tips. A heaping pile of condoms is made in the corner and used to light a bonfire that keeps the restaurant's staff warm until morning.

But Bea sometimes spills drinks. Not often, but sometimes. She works a lot, so she has many opportunities to make mistakes. The simplest error and your day can be ruined. People don't like having drinks spilled on them. A blank stare. Gritted teeth. Angry snarls at home are almost enough to make me feel concerned when she brings the aura of the restaurant back to our house. The prickly, tiny hairs on my neck go up and I feel the charge, the energy of the food-house where she spends countless hours bending over tables to make the money she turns into our food, fun, and shelter.

We sometimes talk about life like we're not living it, she and I. Why? She still works, still lives, and still sees me, *lives with me*: the gas-station attendant college drop-out good-lay boyfriend who now knows that the world's going to end. I haven't told her about that yet. Soon I will. Maybe she'll quit her job too. Maybe she'll go absolutely berserk and climb on the roof. Maybe she'll beg to be fucked by the great positive cosmic force.

I can see it now.

"There's a giant bird in the sky!" she yells.

"That's the police helicopter, Bea. Come inside and put some clothes on. You're going to get arrested. Remember last time?"

"I'm not coming inside. Not until you fill me up. I want every cock in the building. Feed me cock. If you won't do it I'll wait for the cops to drop down here, and I'll fuck one of them."

"That's terrible."

But she doesn't hear me. It doesn't matter where the cock comes from, as long as its stiff.

But I'm being a little harsh.

All she really wants is security. What twisted confusion happens under these tent-like covers, what social conditioning goes on in the bedroom? The history of the world is the history of who fucked whom.

Of course, the days of this stuff are numbered.

Right now it's just she and I. Me and her. Us. Them? I don't know where they are.

I feel her hips grind down on my face. I've stuck a finger inside her ass and am wiggling it around consciously; she enjoys it, and her groan turns into a grunt as she flexes and tenses. I've lines of her juices dribbling down my chin. I lick my lips as she crawls off me, collapsing into the bed at my side. Her face glows from the candlelight. I look closely at her teeth. Her canines are sharp. The light almost blinds me. I stare blankly. Incredible, this... body. Our body. Her body. She opens her eyes and looks at me, no doubt wondering why I've not mounted her by now, like I usually do.

"What's wrong, baby?" she asks, putting out a

hand.

The divine mother.

"The world's going to end in less than nine days."

Her eyes widen a little bit, take on that twisted look I associate with anal rape, two cocks up her begging cunt, debauchery, ass-slapping pain-joy. "That's crazy. Come here."

I feel myself pause. I don't pause for reconsideration: I *know* the world's going to end.

Will she believe me? If I really believed in our *relationship*, I'd try and tell her more. I realize that it's pointless and that I'm disconnected from her anyway. I want to be alone, more than anything, but instead I crawl over to her and put my head on her shoulder. She reaches down and wraps her fingers around my cock. We make a mess over both our stomachs, which she cleans gleefully.

... less than nine days.

I fall asleep in her arms, but I'm not really there. I take off into a world of dreams. I'm comfortable in dreams, usually. It's more like reality, to me. I wander around in a daze, anyway, so why not embrace the permanent daze of drowsy sleep?

I was wrong, of course – everybody's a victim, even if they aren't in a relationship. Maybe that's what is meant by original sin. We know this, all of us, deep down. What we don't know is *why* we're being punished. What crime have we committed in this incarnation? Why us? Why did we fall from that proverbial garden? I'd like to find out, but I know I never will. There's no time.

We fall asleep next to one another without another word. Dreaming, there's no time for me to feel the world, the whale – and myself inside it – slip away. It's just... gone.

Oryoki

8 Days

to remain eating

Noon

A gorgeous heaping plate of Lo Mein noodles stare up at me. A menagerie of sea-green pea-pods, yearning strands of broccoli, arching swoops of sliced carrots, and healthy chunks of beef adorn the plain white plate. I'm in a Chinese restaurant, alone, trying but unable to eat. The food *looks* delicious, but I can't get myself past the sickeningly sweet smell, especially of the beef.

It's strange. A cow dies, and on the way to the table it becomes beef. A carrot dies, and it's still a carrot. A pig dies, and on its way to the table it becomes pork. A deer dies and it becomes venison. Someone digs a potato up, and it's still a potato. A chicken dies... well, it's still chicken. Maybe it has something to do with eating mammals – specifically pigs and cows – which requires the linguistic modification. Obviously we're deluding ourselves.

Tonight Mrs. Billington's daughter will announce her intention to marry Ronald Mill, the son of Gerald Mill, the wealthy architect. The whole family has gathered at Dalio's for a fabulous *meal and some* fabulous *news. Mrs. Billington feels butterflies in her stomach, and she doesn't even have anything to announce! Her daughter told her earlier in the evening about the engagement, and they cried* and cried and cried together. Mrs. Billington hadn't felt that close to her daughter in years. She promised not to tell anybody until the announcement is made.

Mrs. Billington's daughter gives Mrs. Billington a meaningful look and a smile. Mrs. Billington takes a long drink from her white wine and feels it go to her touchy spot, making her feel soft and airy. Mr. Billington is not there to hear the announcement. He is away on business.

Mr. Billington is a serial killer in his spare time. He targets tall young men, whom he rapes and then cuts open with a great Masonic sword. He drinks the fluids from the cuts, believing that he intakes the power and the youth of his young victims with every ounce of their precious moisture. He will be caught within the year and avoid conviction for murder with an insanity plea, along with help from his fellow Masons. The other Billingtons don't know this yet. Their night promises to be peaceful.

"What a beautiful restaurant," Mrs. Billington's friend Anne says.

"Yes, it is," Mrs. Billington replies, startled out of her wine buzz sedation. She hopes the mood is right for her daughter to make the announcement.

A smiling waiter approaches the table with a flourish. The group pauses expectantly while the waiter lays down *their meals. As he lays the trays down he says, "Dead cow? Who has the dead cow. Dead baby cow? Yes, you. Good. And who has the dead pig?"*

Nobody responds.

"Who has the DEAD COW? What about the DEAD PIG? Anybody?"

The night is ruined, and Mrs. Billington doesn't know why. One of the guests mentions something about a poor meal, bad service or such. Mrs. Billington ignores the sour mood and drinks herself into a stupor. She hopes her child has more sense than to marry into a meaningless marriage. The money will be good, though – lots of dead baby sheep to eat and lots of pretty rocks to wear on the neck and on the ears.

There are some things we human animals do for a reason, though we aren't really sure of the particulars. The whole language bit is one of those things. I suppose its useful, but there's so much that occurs underneath it. One of the fundamental misunderstandings about language is that it reveals more than it conceals. I think that's another one of those whale-lies we tell ourselves, to maintain. Because we have to maintain.

I push the plate away and feel disgusted. What's the point of eating if the world's coming to an end? For a moment this morning I thought that all this had been a bad dream and that Bea was right, that I am being crazy, but then I remembered the flash of bright red letters projected onto the wall of the men's room at the gas station:

July 27th at 6:10 P.M.

That had been it, the revelation of the end. I was washing my hands, and inside the mirror the date and time had appeared. Then suddenly I understood what it meant. I had seen it coming for years, had always suspected an imminent end. I always waited for the sign, and I knew this was it. The strange red script lasted inside the mirror for a few seconds. It glowed just so strongly as to block out parts of my face in the reflection, the disappeared to from wherever it came. Something came to me in that moment in the form of a divine flash of insight, and I knew that the end is near. Now I live in limbo, and you do to. We're all just waiting it out. If you think you aren't, you're lying to yourself.

We here in the west have a very pathetic notion of nothingness: we don't. You have to look eastward for any real, practical understand of the cosmic negative.

[T-] 40

Zen monks in Japan traditionally have a set of bowls called Oryoki or "that which contains just enough." They use these bowls when they beg for their food, and the bowls, regardless of whether they are empty or full, are said to contain just what the monk needs.

Right now my bowl is too full. This is not a balanced moment in my life. I feel empty, and I see that the bowl in front of me is quite full, but I can't force the equilibrium to occur – that natural exchange from something to nothing, nothing to something, that should occur between the two forces. I feel hunger, but I also feel ill. Everything symbolizes the end – or an end, depending how bad off – illuminated, cursed – you are – when you're this paranoid.

Echoes ring through my head with every grinding noise to come up from my teeth...

"Judgement... judgement... judgement..." the noises say, and I wonder if the noise from inside or from outside my poor head.

I say the end is near.

Are you ready for that moment, to be sent down the Nile in your lonely raft? Am I?

Paranoid isn't the right word for this, because I am *certain*. Paranoia, for me, always includes a *severe* uncertainty, and that's what makes it *bearable*. I don't enjoy paranoia, but at least when I'm paranoid I know what's happening – I know I have no idea, no control. *Now*, I am sure, am sure that the world is coming to an end, but at an earlier moment I had doubts. I'm being sure to write only when I'm sure of my assertions, because otherwise this would reek of insecurity, and nothing kills a buzz more than an insecure author. That's contradictory, isn't it, to write when you know it won't mean anything, to know you'll never be read. But that's the way I'm working right now. I don't pretend to know why I can do this now but never could before. It's an anomaly of character, perhaps.

Bea left for work around noon, and I was still in bed. I haven't told her that I quit my job. I don't think that I will. What would be the point? If I'm wrong – and that almost seems impossible – then I'm wrong, and I'll find another job. I'll suck it up, go out, swallow my pride, and start pulling in some more of the blood-soaked, oil-soaked American cash. Why not? Everybody's doing it.

I can't imagine what life would be like if I'm wrong and the world's going to keep going, as it is, as it has... since *I* can remember. I've *prepared* myself for

[T-] 42

the end. No. I'm *preparing* myself for the end. I'll never *really* be ready. Who will? I'm aware now of the weird nature of mortality, the finite nature of all things. That one day in the mirror, that one strange sign, devilish or divine... changed me, changed everything around me. How is that possible?

They say that love moves the world, but in this time, for me, everything turns on a single date, one moment in time that I suspect will suspend all possibilities and end us all. Paranoid? Me. No way.

"Finished-uh, sew? Do-eh you wan' a box-uh?" the Chinese waiter asks me. He looks tired. I take a longer look at him and readjust my opinion. I feel tired. He looks bored, but he doesn't look tired. He looks *wired*.

When you're like this, this way I am, you see only your own fear and weakness in the faces of others. Avoid this feeling if you can. Help yourself however you do. Do you cook? Cook well. Do you play basketball? Enjoy that. Do you paint, or write, or sew? Do those things well. Never get like this, because it's worse than being unproductive. It's like having your soul castrated. No, it's like *waiting* to have your soul castrated.

Why bother getting a box? "No thanks." I stand

and throw down a ten dollar bill – which amounts to quite a large tip for the wired waiter – then step around the corner.

I haven't slept well for a few days. This is not a surprise. I'm afraid that if I fall asleep I'll miss the end. I know that's absurd – who can sleep for a week? – but I just can't force myself to rest. I've been thinking a lot about those moments of absolute darkness when you're asleep but aren't dreaming, aren't conscious of *anything*: absolute rest moments. It always seemed desirable to sleep like that before I woke up to the end. Now that same darkness that once comforted petrifies me. I'm afraid of falling too far asleep. I want to wake up, and I'm afraid if I slip too far, I'll lose it forever.

If only I hadn't discovered this truth, this date, this *burden*, I wouldn't be on this weird walk – not this walk down the street to the coffee house, but the metaphorical walk through these last, wasted days of the universe's existence. Does that make sense? If I didn't know about the coming end would I be going through this? No. I'd still work at the gas station. I'd still visit Bea at her restaurant. I might even consider going back to college or picking up a pencil to draw once in a while. I might care about music, or clothes, or credit-cards, or current affairs, or soccer games, or the hunger that gnaws at my belly... and the food left behind.

Two smiling monks sit at a wooden table and stare calmly at one another. One of them is large and round and jolly like the typical statue of a Buddha. The other is thin to the point of emaciation. Both smile serenely. The fat monk has a bowl that's full of rice and vegetables. The thin monk has a bowl that's entirely empty. Behind them is a tree full of great, green leaves, beautiful and healthy.

"Well, I guess it's about that time," the fat monk says lazily.

"Yes, it seems to be," the other monk replies, peaceful.

The round monk lifts his bowl and dumps the contents into the thin monk's bowl. Suddenly the leaves of the tree behind them turn from green to golden yellow, then slowly fall from the tree. The leaves fall steadily until not one remains.

A quick moment passes while the tree is leafless, then it begins to bud, and only another moment flows by before the tree is in full bloom again, as before. The thin monk's body, as the tree changes, contorts and takes on all the features of the fat monk's, while the fat monk's body grows thin and matches his colleague's form.

"I'm glad that's over," the now-thin monk says, peaceful.

Where do these things – these visions – come from that pass through my brain? I jot them down because they're a part of this, but I don't know why. I'm in the coffee house now. They're playing some kind of shifty music, calm but aggressive with some strong female vocals, rock that uses a violin. It's nice enough to tolerate. I sit down on a couch without ordering coffee. That's the last thing I need right now, caffeine to keep me more wide awake, to give me *more* clarity. I *need* a sedative.

I look around the familiar coffee shop. This is one of those places for graduate students to sit around and play chess, mouth off to each other and pretend to care about important topics relevant to the socially aware youth of today. Heil to the Academy. Goddamn does it make me tired, to think of all the worthless papers these poor kids – what am I saying? Some of them are older than me – write for their courses.

I eavesdrop on a conversation. Two guys, young, white, they look like brothers – might be – talk to each other, probably about college.

"You can be an engineer. You know. You can be a 'this' and you can be a 'that'. But there's a limit to the things you can be. You know. Things you can be... all listed in a single page," the younger one says, black hair curled over the front of his face.

"What does that have to do with eating?" asks the older one, straight-haired, blond. He has a deep voice, like a father's.

"Because there's only one job really. *Survive.* That's why there aren't many choices. Like I always thought there would be so many different kinds of jobs, so many different things. And there *isn't.*"

That's insightful, I think, oozing sarcasm to myself. I shift way back into the couch and try to melt into the seat. I don't want to think about the fleeting wastefulness of even the slightest movement.

I have a theory: without coffee houses there would not be angst. Coffee houses *create* angst. Before the coffee house, people were happy. It's a pet theory, but it just might be the answer. I zone in on the conversation again.

"Ultimately it boils down to being a *human,*" the older one answers.

Right. Very insightful. You knob.

"I just thought there was more."

Forget about it. In eight days there will be less than nothing. It's pathetic to cling to all these things, desperate to make sense out of something you'll never understand. This is my sublime position. I'm like the monks beneath the tree, because I know about the wax and wane, the absurdity of finality.

"There probably is. You're just looking at..."

The younger one cuts him off. "I want to do something in a studio. I want to make *music*! I want to be the official person who puts in input. I'd like to be the official suggestor... and then leave, get paid for it. I would do this."

"What about music production?"

"I don't know."

"Isn't that what a producer does?" the older one asks.

"I'd just like to be a musician... I'm not worried about the sound. Like... I don't freak out if a drum doesn't sound right."

"I think that's a way for people to avoid learning about the soul of music."

"I'd just like to be a musician. That's impossible. Where are you going to go? What are you going to do? I can drum, I can sing, I can play piano... Trumpet. But it's just like a fine art. Like painting. Who would want to study that?"

"Just go off and do your own thing."

"I would like to meet a producer. Y'know what I mean?"

"I don't."

"Oh. I'd love to sit down in front of someone, play some piano, sing a little bit... have them say 'I like that. Let's record this.'"

"That's not how it operates," the older brother says.

The younger brother stares upward as the music being played over the coffee house's speakers swells, then says, "I like this music."

Suddenly the younger brother looks very round, and the older brother looks very thin.

What could I say to these two? The young one, just trying to get a grip on the world around him. He probably just moved out. The older one, who's about my age, is just old enough to be *jaded*, but he's no better. His grip is no more firm than his younger siblings. And what *could* I say to make things better? If I butted in, I'd have nothing to submit to their conversation except what – to them – would sound insane.

There's so much misplaced hope in the world. It's all a defense mechanism against terrible, physical truths – like finality, mortality. Misplaced hope is the human organisms defense against eternity.

I feel slightly dizzy. I stand up and stumble out of the coffee house. It's raining. The rain hits my head and my face but only lightly. It's getting dark, and Bea should be home by now. I feel an intense need to explain myself, and she's as close to me as anyone I'll never know.

**Glory Stream
7 Days
In-Between-Time**

Even now while I dream I feel thirsty. Though my consciousness floats around in visions, I feel a deep bodily need for drink. Despite this parched feeling I have, I can't wake from this dream state. I float around in a green abyss.

I glance suddenly to the right, where I see something black. The black thing shifts away from my vision as I move my head.

What the hell? I think.

I momentarily forget my thirst. This is the hierarchy of needs in action. Does thirst come before something large and dark floating dangerously close to your head? Not for me.

I blink a few times – or I feel like I do. I'm dreaming, so I can't know – and get a quick flash of a crab, the moon, and a child.

Abort all fetus – no progeny. Sacrifice all children and back always away from birth-rebirth action, like the crab. Move backwards like the crab. That way you will always know where you're going, because the past doesn't change. That sounds reasonable. Going forward is too risky. You might tumble headlong into a terrible abyss and never wake up. Then who would play drums for the world?

All our hearts are beating. Endless drums. Endless drumming. Thrum thrum thrum. Bump-be-bump.

I look all around the right side of my head, but there's no sight of the black *thing* which caught my attention. All I see are huge green shapes spread out for what seems forever, shifting blobs like the interior of a lava lamp.

Another black object seems to shift past me, but this time it moves on the left and doesn't disappear. It's *connected* to me, comes out of my head and arches upward and away. It's a great ethereal horn, and as I roll my astral – astral? dream? sleep? – eyes upward to try and hone in on the details, I realize that illusive thing to the right is a similar bony growth.

"I have horns...?" I half ask myself, half state this aloud. It's difficult to ask questions of yourself, especially when you don't know who or what you are.

I think I hear a trumpet's blast.

The word "Esiach" appears at my feet in a controlled, black script. I almost forget about the horns protruding out of my head. The word rises up from the unreal green ground and slides up my left leg.

The two brothers from yesterday? Esiach, brother, Enoch... These things sound familiar, but I don't know why?

Seven days to live, seven nights to dream.

This is not your normal dream. What inspires this? Normally I think about food or sex while I'm asleep... or whales, giant whales... something, anything less convoluted. I rarely remember my dreams. This one is becoming more complicated.

The scenery around me starts moving – I don't move. I must make this clear. I don't move. It's like a video game. You know that when you press a button on the controller you aren't controlling the character. You control the screen's movement in relation to the character. It's like that. But you believe the illusion anyway, and so do I. The game isn't fun if you don't.

Six mountains float past me, each with a different river or stream that flows around or over it. The streams are all filled with different colored water, orange, red, green, blue, yellow, white – ghostly but still *present*. Sensations of boiling heat and icy cold accompany them, run up from my feet till the great battle between hot and cold bubbles over and reaches up through my neck into my head. A large black spire appears, the seventh mountain. It draws so close that I roll my eyes back into my head to see the heights which loom over me. I never discover how high the thing goes before my vision blacks out, but I realize that the peak is a third horn which spirals out of the center of my head.

I feel a burning, then a freezing cold. My head goes numb – a sensation which appeals to me. I hear a soft buzzing noise. This lasts for an indefinite length of time before I again open my dream's eyes and see to where I have come.

I don't want to mislead you in this description. Writing this, I make it sound as if I have an element of control in this dreaming. It's like the heat and the cold. Sometimes I feel warm, like I have control, and sometimes I feel cold like I'm completely being swept away.

One never knows, though, if it is only an illusion of control. Ultimately, we convince ourselves of free will or we don't. In dreams it is easy to be swept away by the extreme feelings of control... or loss of.

I'm sitting at the edge of a stream. I'm underground. When I stand I hear the noise of my motion's echo. My surroundings are dark, but there is some light. It comes from a shining point downstream. Despite the blackness, I make out some things that moves in the water. I can't quite make out what they are – *probably some kind of fish,* I think – so I decide to move toward the light.

As I move my vision of the things that swim around in the stream improves. Symbols, the hieroglyphs of a dozen different languages, sigils, and geometric patterns of all shapes and sizes fill this strange stream to overflowing. The stream itself *consists* of these patterns. I stare in awe as a batch of Hebrew letters floats past me, followed closely by a strange kind of hexagram, not the usual kind one sees, with a bright red rose that blooms in its center.

How do I know these things? They're being put into my mind. Is the stream my mind? It's dark. I can't tell the difference.

Words float in the stream, as if reading my thoughts, "Your horns are gone."

I reach up quickly and grope at my head. I expect to feel horns. I don't. Instead I feel a shaved scalp, which is strange because in my waking life I have a ratty head of hair. I don't even shampoo.

Before I even realize I've thought the question, the stream answers it. Amidst the symbols I read, "You're *inside* one of the horns, so you don't need them now. You're safe. If you could see them..." The text becomes garbled here as a large ✝ passes in the current and scrambles the sentence. I pick up the thought, reading, "... make a symbol for protection. See? ♀ "

A blank moment passes.

"You need to learn to be more careful with those horns. Sometimes you hurt people when you bump into them. You have to learn how to avoid that. If you find *your* path, you won't ever really cause meaningless suffering. Don't you wonder about the light?"

As a matter of fact, I do.

But I don't say it. I can't bring myself to talk with a stream. How do you communicate with words themselves? I don't know.

I feel, for a moment, like the ground beneath me has disappeared, and I stumble.

"Better get moving," the letters say. Then I see an ⇨ . It points in the direction of the light.

The stream has insulted my intelligence.

"Thanks," I mutter, speaking to the stream for the first time. The word, as it comes out of my mouth, creates a splash in the water, and I watch it float downstream, a red mass of letters in a stream of blue.

I walk in the direction of the light. The stream flows by my side, and I make a point of ignoring whatever it tries to tell me. It makes my head hurt, the stream. The very idea of it is offensive, and beyond that, it's difficult to read the English amidst all the other garbled symbols anyway.

It doesn't take long for me to reach the light. I stand now between two large stone pillars. The stream flows through the center of these pillars and into a large temple. I look upward and try to sense the true proportions of where I'm heading, but there's no ceiling – very strange – and no way to gauge. There is, however, a floor, which consists of large red and green squares, like the bottom of a chess board but colored differently. There are forty-nine squares. I quickly count seven by seven. The stream disappears beneath the chess-board-style grid.

The center squares of the floor are made of a large square altar. Inside the altar, which is made of some kind of black metal, rests a lamp, from which emanates the soft light. Bea sits atop the altar, but I've never seen her like this before. She's radiant, dressed in flowing white robes, and her eyes look like they never have before – gleaming and intelligent and benign, magnificent in every way. Her robes are so thin that I can see her nakedness beneath them as I approach the altar, stunned. The scar beneath her breast is gone.

"The moon has four faces. There are seven days for each," Bea says.

It might not be right to say that it's Bea speaking to me in this dream, this vision, but for some reason it feels like she is – like maybe her soul is talking to me in this dream. Is that possible?

She smiles. It looks eerie but also beautiful, wonderful, like she conceals a million secrets. "You have four faces. You never show them, dreamspeaker."

I think... what? As I do, I hear myself say, "What?"

If my waking life were like this and I said everything I thought, I'd ask "why" and "what" a lot more often. I wonder why I don't.

"You're like the moon. You have four faces. You never show them, though. You're an infinite eclipse."

This sparks something deep inside of me – no surprise. The stream told me that already, in its way. For the first time in a long time I feel a real emotional range, a strange twist of energy that ascends from my gut and wraps around my chest. My heart beats out a steady rhythm, a big warm bass drum in the center of my frail chest.

"If there was anybody worth showing," I spit, "then I'd show them something." My own venom surprises me. It's so strange, to surprise yourself.

Bea – this beautiful dream-phantom – doesn't respond. Now I'm positive this isn't the Bea I know, because the Bea I know would shriek and tell me what kind of a bastard I am. This one only smiles.

I feel abashed, life a child in front of a holy person... proven wrong and made small. Poor little weak, stupid me.

"Reach inside and take the lantern." Her eyes are deep streams. I can almost see symbols running through them.

A sudden thought comes into my mind, and I realize that this must be Bea. This is the Star of Bea – before any moment, before reality, after time, between everything, *this is how she is*: radiant, virginal, pure, sublime... a star.

What a complete rush.

She spreads her legs to either side of the alter, but the motion doesn't seem lewd or sexual. Sex is the last thing on my mind as I walk toward the lantern – and, by mentioning it, it's also the first thing on my mind, but it isn't what I normally associate with sex. Maybe there are two types of sex... two aspects to sex.

Of course there are. That's fundamental. When we don't see the two, we're dwelling in a closed box... like the lantern inside the altar. I see that now.

Altar – Alter. Hmm...

I reach inside and pull out the lamp. It is shaped like a pyramid without the top peak. It tapers off an inch too soon. It has no handle, so I hold it from underneath. It is about the length of a person's navel to the nipple, no more than a foot and a half. There is warmth but no real danger to the heat. I realize that there is a flame beneath the light, but it seems unreal: it casts too much light for such a small flame. It has no source.

"Open it," the Star of Bea demands without sounding demanding.

So I do. I reach over to one of the lamps corners and pull the glass aside. It moves like a latch, though there's no hinge and no physical reason for it to move. It doesn't startle me. Nothing much could startle me right now. I'm pretty well blown away.

I reach out my hand and pull the flame from the pyramid lantern. I hold the flame in the palm of my hand and, impetuously, place it up to my forehead.

I'm actually holding the flame. I feel it wrap up and around the little cracks and creases of my hand, warm and wonderful. It should be hot, but it's not. It feels fantastic.

The flame sinks inside of me, into my forehead, and I feel an intense heat burrow deep into its new home, deep between the lobes of my brain.

I'm sure I heard a trumpet blast.

Solar Tentatio
6 Days
Noon

Wake up, and let it go.

A brief moment of clarity sweeps over me, an absolutely lucid insight: the world is not coming to an end. I'm a paranoid. I'm absolutely delusional. Everything must be okay, because if things weren't okay, I never would have had such a beautiful dream.

How do you go on with your life after a dream like that? Do you keep living as you always have? Do you record the memory of the thing and try to tear it apart, deconstruct the image until you have an understanding, until you stand beneath it and can see what occurred? Or do you let the dream integrate into your daily life, let it become like a mantra, run over and over again in your mind until you can draw it up at any moment. I don't know. *I've never had a dream like that before.*

When the feeling of clarity passes I become suddenly conscious of my body and an intense heat. I'm sweating. The sheets are soaked with it, with *me*, endless rivulets, endless streams of my moisture. Real awareness eludes me. The most I can feel is ill. I know *something* is wrong. I wish it weren't. I wish I could hold the moment, stretch it.

Something's being pushed to my lips. It's a glass of water. I drink from it slowly. Some water spills over onto my bare chest. My hair feels sticky and disgusting.

I remember the shaved feeling from the dream. I think I'll do that soon, before the world ends. I want to go out with a clean scalp.

Now when I think of the end I see fire. I reach a hand up and rub my forehead. I can still feel the heat. It's *inside* me. I can't rub it away. I'm pregnant with it, with the flame. What's it going to do to me?

When I open my eyes I see Bea through the afternoon grogginess. The clock says that it's 12:01. It feels like morning. Bea looks down at me. Her nostrils seem to be large in a very unholy way. I can see right up them into a cavernous darkness. I try not to laugh. She doesn't look pleased.

"How long have I slept?" I groan.

"You were in bed when I came home last night."

"When was that?"

"Seven."

"Jesus," I say. I try to sit up, but Bea puts a patronizing hand on my forehead and holds me down.

"You were groaning in your sleep. I couldn't make out all of what you were saying, but I know I heard you say 'judgement.' You have a fever."

"Is that it? I feel like I've been run over." I reach out and grab for the glass, from which I gladly drink. The water feels like cool, shiny silver, running down my throat. It helps, but I still feel incredibly dizzy.

The terror of my knowledge is surpassed only by

my fear of Bea. She gives me a long, bitter look. I feel low. I remember her from the dream. I don't think I'll ever look at her in the same way again.

Something *definitely* has to change, even if I only have six days to make it happen. Can I do that? When's the last time I tried to change? If the world ends and I'm still a pathetic geek, will I be immortalized as pathetic and miserable? Is the end concrete or fluid? These are fundamental questions, especially when the end grows nigh.

Why is she looking at me like that?

"I knew you had to work this morning, so I called Virgil to let him know that you're sick..." she mumbles.

Now I know why she's looking at me like that.

She turns away from me. She picks some clothes from the foot of the bed and tosses them into the corner. She shuffles around the room, stepping over and around the scattered messes. We have a large bedroom, but there's only one real path from the door to the bed. Our junk clutters the rest of the room.

"I work almost every day," she says, facing away from me. She turns back suddenly. "I'm trying to get into *college*. How are we going to pay for everything if only *I* work? This place is *expensive*."

I try to sit up but can't. It's difficult to move. I

feel like something heavy is trying to open itself out of my stomach and my forehead. I reach down and do a system's check. Dizzy, I start to panic as I twist my hand around my stomach and groin. It feels like I have two cocks. I blink a few times, then moan again.

What the hell is happening to me?

Bea stops long enough to stare at me. A moment of sympathy comes over her, and she leans at the bedside. "What's *wrong*?"

"The world's coming to an end," I mutter. I realize I sound like a child.

"That's insane," she says. She puts a comforting hand on my head and strokes it a few times. "Do you really think that?"

"Yes."

"Is that why you quit your job?"

"Yes."

She stands and yells, "You're a fucking lunatic!" She moves more furiously than I've *ever* seen her move. She grabs her backpack and a bottle of water. "I can't believe you. What do I always say? You're not motivated to do *anything*. That damned job was about the only *solid* thing that gets you out of this place. It would be different if you did something around here, or even if you gave a good fuck..."

Ouch.

"... but you don't fucking well *do* anything. It's like you're sleep-walking. I don't have time to take care of you today. I have to *work*," she snarls. "God fucking damnit. God damn shit fucking damnit. You whore of a man."

"You weren't working," I mumble, "when I met you. You didn't even have a place to say."

As soon as I say this, I know it was a mistake. Before the words even flow from my lips, I know I've fucked myself. But I don't care.

She looks like a volcano. She *is* a volcano. This is not a comparison. This is truth. She bubbles, boils, explodes, shifts, moves, *roars*, "But I'm working *now*. And I'm *sane*, you fucking maniac."

Part of me is laughing. *Sane?* This female animal in front of me, screaming like a banshee, with eyes aflame in demonic wrath... is sane?

"You don't *sound* sane."

Her energy deflates some as she hisses loudly, "I have to go to *work*." She gives me the most disappointed look as she says, "You can explain this to me when I get back. You had *better* explain this to me when I get back." She stares at me, then adds, like an afterthought, "*If* I come back." She leaves the room with her things. I hear the front door of our apartment close. I listen to her lock the door with a snap.

[T-] 67

The window to our room is open. A shaft of sunlight glares down on me, across the bed and over my face. I throw the sheets from over me and roll over. I squint my eyes at the light and hold them closed. I see red spots.

The redness turns in an instant to black, and I open my eyes. To the left of the bed, between me and the window, stands a tall, pale person. I can't say whether it's a man or a woman. It's bald, absolutely hairless. It is pale to the point of whiteness and has clear, colorless eyes. It wears a cashmere sweater and a dark pair of pants, and it's smiling calmly. Through the back of its pants swings a four-foot tail, snakelike and pointed at the end. The tail has a thin layer of phosphorescent scales which give off a strangely attractive glow that momentarily mesmerizes me.

I roll back to the other side of the bed.

Ignore the imp, or whatever it is, on the other side. Forget about the terrible fact that something's inside the room and enjoy one of the last moments of consciousness you'll ever have. Six days of fun, fun, fun in the sun, sun, sun.

"Ahem," the thing says. It does not clear it's throat. It literally says, "Ahem." It would have a good singing voice were it inclined to sing.

I open my eyes are stare at the wall. This thing will not be ignored. There is a pregnant pause which I don't try to break. What can I say? How do you speak to the thing by the bed with the glowing tail and the nightmare eyes? It sound like a teacher.

"Ahem."

Nothing. Ignore it. Just ignore it.

"Hello, light-bearer," the thing says solemnly. I roll over and stare up at it, moving my eyes but not my head. I'm so tired. The creature steadily returns my stare. I glance away, then it shakes its head. "You speak the American language, yes?"

"Yeah," I say into my pillow. "I guess you could say I speak 'American.'"

"Oh good," it says. It sits down on the end of the bed. I can feel my feet sink a little bit as its weight bends the mattress. "I'd hate to have to rip off your head and give you a new Lingo."

"What?"

"Never mind. It's not important." The speech has suddenly become much more familiar, almost paternal... maternal... ternal.

Is that a word? It should be. Parental. Yes.

I turn over and look down to the foot of the bed. The creature is looking around the room. "What a mess," it says, no doubt referring to the wall to wall clutter of our bedroom, plates and dishes stacked up and left to rot. "I've seen the great spiral labyrinth where the guts of the damned are torn and set upon by malicious ifrit. I have witnessed eternal torment, an endless flowing river of the unconscious sufferers who dwell in their own bilious excrement, unimaginable pits of scatologically nightmarish gore and vomitous waste, spiceless Chinese food every night, endless galleries of modern art!" it crescendoes in a dramatic rise, then more quietly says "but *this* takes the cake. What confuses me is why you would live like this when you have a choice.

I'm being lectured by somebody more fucked up than I am.

"That's what you'll never understand," it goes on. "You really *do* have a choice. It's fantastic, all the noise that your philosophers produce to cover up the simple fact of free will. Do you know why I think most all you humans are determinists?"

God. God. God. I feel like I'm dying, and this invader wants to discuss metaphysics.

"I'll tell you why," it says vehemently. It's tail flies into the air, lands with a dull thud on the edge of my bed. "Because the notion of free-will terrifies you little bipeds, as well it should. You think that God made you in his *physical* image, that God looks like a human? That's a disgusting notion. God made you *free* in his image." The thing shakes his head again, then chews on its lower lip ponderously.

"Who the *hell* are you?" I ask, pulling the pillow from over my head.

It replies in the solemn voice from before. Beneath the words I can almost hear the screams of a billion damned, tortured souls... in my bedroom. "I am called many things. Prince of the Fallen. God of Ekron. Be'ezlebub, Lord of the Flies, Foremost Prince of the Dark Angels, Supreme Bearer of Light, Lord of Calumny, and The Master of Diabolism. I have a PhD in Psychology from Stanford and am involved in many community groups and activities. I'm also a practicing Freemason."

It pauses to flick some lint off its lovely cashmere sweater. It looks over at a stack of my compact discs and asks, "You like Led Zeppelin?"

I slowly sit up. I figure I might as well get straight to the point. Why bother asking *how* this *thing* got into my apartment? I've probably slipped into a dream again, or one of my dreams has slipped into reality. Either way, the fastest way to end the nightmare is to ride it out. I hope. "You could probably tell me why the world's going to end in six days, if you are who you say you are," I say.

"That's such a complicated question, light-bearer," it says. "There are many kinds of ends and beginnings, many kinds of falls and ascensions. Your American language is a very limited one. It keeps you from expressing the full range of possibilities. *All* language is inherently flawed, but with yours, it's almost impossible to order a good *meal* – impossible, actually, in St. Paul. Do you know Greek?"

"I don't know Greek."

"Well, to the early Greeks, the word 'apocalypse' originally meant a revelation."

"Like the book in the Bible?"

"Something like that," the thing says. Its tail moves around the bed. "Do you know that the word 'lucifer' means 'one who gives light'?"

"No, I didn't know that," I say, feeling ill. "Look..." I go on, annoyed at this invasion of my metaphysical space. "I didn't ask for you to come here. I thought people had to summon you or something like that."

"Your girlfriend managed to build up enough energy – a wide enough door, so to speak – so it was easy for me to get in. Besides, I would have gotten to you eventually today. It's fated – yes, free will and fate can coincide – to happen. You have a great light in your head now, and it's important for all parties concerned that it gets out. This includes your god."

"My god?"

"Your better self. Your ideal. Whatever. Look. I have souls to torture who have *lost* their sense of guilt. I

[T-] 72

see that yours is still active and functioning. As long as you have your own sense of guilt, there's *nothing* I can do to torture you more than you already torture yourself."

"You're doing a fine job," I say.

It smiles. Its teeth are absolutely terrifying. Its tongue is forked. I'm glad when it closes its mouth.

"Your tail is showing," I say, choking on my own pathetic attempt at humor. *Your tail is showing?*

Maybe it's not a good idea to taunt a demon. Then again, maybe they like it. They would be the S and M types, wouldn't they? Whips and chains and leather and hellfire – these things seem like they naturally belong to the lower planes. Or maybe that's heaven. It's probably relative. What isn't?

"I've read what you've written. It's quite spare, so far, isn't it? You aren't afraid of letting people know what kind of a bastard you are, now that you know they'll never read it. Hmm?"

"You might be the only one reading it, then, yeah. That wouldn't surprise me," I say. "I don't expect anyone to believe me, and what could they do if they did? Nothing. There's nothing we can do, and I don't care if anybody thinks I'm a bastard. They'll all be gone, anyway. Right?"

"You haven't been listening. Sometimes humans misunderstand messages that are given to them, gifts revealed in visions and such. There is an exterior meaning and an interior meaning in *everything*. *We're* good at seeing both, because we are the ones who give light. You guys aren't quite so good at it, because your light really isn't your own to carry. You carry a flame now, too. You remember your dream? I read that entry. Maybe you should learn how to use a colon."

And now it wants to talk about my grammar.

Or something worse.

"We've been really disappointed lately in the quality of your species' literary ability. We used to get some respect from your storytellers. Goethe, Lewis, Dante... even Crowley – these were men of character, of wit, of *grace!*" The thing snorts through its nose, then shrugs. "Alas... things aren't what they used to be."

That's for damned sure. "If you don't mind, I'd like to get back to unconsciousness. If you can't answer my question, and you aren't here to sign a contract or something, could you please get out of my apartment?"

The thing actually looks offended, like it's not used to being sent away. It even looks a little *hurt*. "I already answered your question. Let those who can read the signs, read." It stands up and moves back to the shaft of light from whence it came.

"I still don't understand."

"That's okay, neither do I. That's why I'm from

hell."

"Oh yeah... Mmm. That sucks."

"It's not so bad. Rent's cheap, and we never have to pay for heat. Hey," it says, flicking its tail. "Remember what I said. And this too: when the eagle and the dragon join in union, something occurs on the inside of the egg. When it bursts forth the spirit of light and life is experienced as a miracle. If you recognize the miracle for what it is, you achieve grace, if you don't, you... won't." It shrugs.

"Great," I say, laying back in bed. The lecture's almost over. "That makes total sense." Sarcasm.

"'With great knowledge comes great suffering. With great wisdom comes great pain,'" it quotes.

Then it disappears as quickly as it appeared, and I've fallen back into unconsciousness.

When I wake up I come to my feet without hesitation. It must be later in the afternoon, because the sunbeam no longer falls over the bed. I look at the clock: 4:09. I've slept far too long. The fire in my head has moved downward and into my body, out to my limbs. I feel energized.

I look around the room and squint. This place is a mess. It will have to be cleaned. I go into the bathroom and look into the mirror. *I'm* a mess. I undress and look at myself. I am reassured that I only have my one, familiar, well-used cock. It's equally nice see that I have neither a tail nor horns. I get into the shower and let the water wash away the sweat and grime. I get out, dry off, brush my teeth, then pull out my electric razor. I shave my ratty hair from my head and take a straight razor to my scalp. I look like a different person. I get back into the shower to wash the hair away. It feels nice on my clean head.

I spend the next hour cleaning the bedroom. Beneath a pile of plates and old pizza boxes I discover my old drawing pad. I stop cleaning and take the large pad and a pencil upstairs and outside. I sit on the front steps in the fading light. Our apartment is near a large wall that blocks sound off from the terrible highway traffic. Normally it's an eyesore, but tonight the sun setting over the wall casts a glorious orange gleam against the city's skyline.

Once the pencil hits the pad, I sink down into myself. It takes me just a few minutes to sketch out the form of the thing I met earlier. The tail, the bald hair, the eyes, the strange smile – everything comes from the pencil in confidence and seems correct, even when I know I'm making mistakes.

[T-] 76

Later I will paint this.

Tonight I need to talk with Bea. She's not going to believe who I talked with today, but that doesn't matter. There's a chasm between us that I feel like I can bridge. I still feel terrified. I don't understand how the end can be anything but the end. Is there some secret I'm missing?

When I'm satisfied with how the sketch looks, I return to the apartment. I listen to Led Zeppelin's "Kashmir" as I finish cleaning the apartment. I wait for Bea to come home.

I sit now in the living room and look at the sketch, listening as I do to an old Dizzy Gillespie album.

Genum Hominum Perfectum
5 Days
5:55 AM

The New Gospel, Declared After the Fact:

In the middle... there is confusion, a great heaping deal of confusion .

There is so much confusion that the people pour milk into their bowls before they pour their cereal.

People call out "Bingo" before they have bingo.

People wear ties around t-shirts and "I'm With Stupid" t-shirts beneath suits.

People wear fall colors in the spring.

What's worse, people created and living in the great cosmic momentary now don't know how to get along with one another. They bark at each other while driving, can't look one another in the eye, and fear constantly for themselves and constantly fear others.

Great teachers have come to them to explain the relative nature of time, the circular nature of time, the spiral nature of time – anything but the linear nature of time, but they never listen, have never listened, and don't show any indication of opening their ears. Still their clocks tick and tock, and on the inside they try desperately to make their hearts beat to the time of the quartz drummer. But it will never happen. The heart does not beat in time with a clock, can't be contained like that. It beats irregular – within a range, yes, but never predictably. And so they fight, mostly against themselves... always against nature.

That's where I am: right in the middle. Stuck on the middle of the tree, nailed between a set of spinning, static circles, a contradiction-of-itself kind-of-a-thing. Man – free – stuck, slammed onto the tree and nailed firm. What can you do? Whine about it? Cut the tree down?

This tree will not be cut down. A blade set to it releases blood – mostly your own.

Between X and Z there is a Y.

X in this equation was when I discovered the date, **July 27th at 6:10 at night.** Y is the moment. Z is now, the spaces in between that first recognition of revelation and that final moment of apocalypse.

When you have eleven days until apocalypse, the sixth day forms the top arch of all your life's possibilities. Everything around you becomes a huge rock on a dangerously steep sledding hill. Intense despair billows from the inside – your personal pillows become permanently lumpy – so that you become like that archetypical, cosmic cancer patient. You stare off into space for long stretches of time. Clouds begin to look like tumors. Moles begin to look like tumors. Neighbors begin to look suspicious and terrible.

All the television you've watched comes back to haunt you, all those hours wasted staring at a box that, for all you know, might be the very *reason* you're dying.

All the sick vampires that have sucked the joy out of your daily life begin to smell like you imagine your own coffin will, and you see all things through the glaring light of truth and thus *virtuously*. You are benign and above the world, and you project that onto your disease.

"It's benign," you say to yourself about your cancer, reassure yourself... but the question nags, "For how long? How long do I have to waddle around this rock with only myself as company? How many more long and lonely days will I pretend to understand things I'll never know?"

Consciousness is built so that it *recognizes* experience, re-cognates it, re-thinks it, re-lives it. No experience – nothing – nowhere – nobody – these negative concepts boggle the mind and can really plague you, if you let them. An illness descends upon the soul, unless you're prepared with some sort of strong buffer against the despair. Who is? I wasn't... will never be. I don't want to be. I don't want that responsibility. I'm too unprepared for it. At least when I'm without responsibility, I can't be blamed for anything serious.

Cancer. The crab. Closeness. Crawling backwards.

So then the relatives begin to come around. They all express their regrets, send cards, while behind your vision they silently wonder who will get most out of your will. You, in your suddenly lengthy and terrifying spare time, browse the obituaries and compare your life to everybody elses'. How does yours stack up? Think of all the biographies and autobiographies you've read, all the films you've seen about the lives of famous and important and insane people. Where do you fit on the historical geography of humanity, the grand sweeping multidimensional construction we create in our minds? Were you left or right, peace or war, art or business, clean or dirty? Were you somewhere in the middle, part of the gap generation? Can *anybody* be described so simply?

I imagine my own article would read something like this:

A twenty-three year old male of German descent was killed when he was crushed by a large truck with a huge inverted pentagram drawn on its back. Nobody knows where the truck came from or who was driving it. People with information about such a truck should contact the police as soon as possible.

The victim died clutching a weird - presumably self-drawn - sketch of what appears to be deceased occultist Aleister Crowley. Crowley could not be reached for a comment because he's well and dead - good riddance. No connection between the self-proclaimed "Beast 666" and the victim have yet been discovered, though various theories of the conspiratorial sort have been forwarded by friends of the victim and members of the press.

The victim, who recently left his job at a local gas station, where fellow employees described him as 'a quiet loner with a pension for pornography'. 'He was particularly interested in the human anatomy. He was a queer duck,' said a fellow attendant.

'But that's a shame, y'know? To get hit by a truck. Who'd want to go out like that? I want to die slowly in the hospital.'

The victim did absolutely nothing with his life, as far as anybody at this newspaper can tell, and if he hadn't been killed in a freak accident, nobody would be interested at all in his leaving this planet. He is survived by a girlfriend he's never really loved and parents from whom he's grown distant.

We looked for somebody else to interview, but because this person was so incredibly meaningless, we decided to just skip it and save the space. Thank you.

                                    - The

Editors

If you think your obituary would, if you were hit by a truck, read something like this, you're one of the select few: the People without Promise. People without Promise, unite under one banner. We might be able to achieve something. We'll be *very* sure to avoid dictators after we organize, won't we? Why repeat the mistakes of our ancestors? Let's one up them. Let's make dictators out of ourselves. Everybody has value! Let everyone dictate!

Hmm. On second thought, it might be better, in fact, if we don't organize and instead stay separate until we all actually *show* some promise. That way, when we get together, we'll have something to talk about rather than the weather, cars, or why one band is better than the other. Right? Right.

Die quickly. It's not worth waiting around. Die daily, because otherwise you'll start to pick up a really, really bad smell. Good advice, if you're able to distinguish between subtle layers of meaning and pure crap. Pure crap – that's a notion I don't want to dig around in. Tutamuka. Tutamuka. Pure crap. Between the lines there might be something. I don't know. I haven't looked yet, can't stand to. I want to take everything literally. It's so much easier that way, so much more safe and tight and well-wrapped. No questions.

But I can't. So I won't.

Death and rebirth are two parts to the same concept. The body recycles all of its cells every seven years, even as it remains living and we *feel* a continuity in ourselves. We *molt*. What a concept.

We... fucking... *molt*. Shed skin.

Somebody said once that every important decision should be made in the span of seven breaths. Good advice, I think. It keeps you from over-thinking, from dwelling on one thing for too long.

There are seven cardinal virtues and there are seven deadly sins. There were seven dwarves. There are seven days of the week. Seven blasts from the trumpet. Seven is the number of Venus. Seven days from the end of the world, I was given a vision in a dream, saw a place beautiful and expansive. Every so often I check to see if I have horns.

Six days before the end of the world I think I might have sold my soul to the devil. I'm not sure. He didn't have me sign anything.

A landlord once told me that only written contracts are binding. Did I make a verbal agreement? He called me a "light-bearer." What the hell does that mean?

Did I sell my soul?! I'm fucked if I did.

This is the fifth day... very early on the fifth day. While we're on numbers, we might as well mention that most every person has five digits on each of their four limbs. We have five physical senses. The Jackson Five... Hmm. Didn't the first part of the Bible come in five books? This might be a numerological anomaly worth analyzing.

But probably not.

Bea and I sometimes laugh when we finish each other's sentences. We share an understanding between the two of us that most definitely transcends the physical. I'm certain of it. There's something between us that can't be contained by the body alone. There's too much happening in the energy.

I know this, after the dream of the Star Bea. There's so much more to her than I could even imagine, so much more than I could ever know.

Are two people together a sum of their parts, or is there some sort of exponential factor we can include in the equation that involves multiplication? Does a couple have ten possibilities for sensation when they're together, or do they have twenty five? Does it depend on how well they work together as a unit, how long they've known each other, or some other factors? Maybe between the X of one person's soul and the Z of another's, there's a Y that might be called the soul of the relationship. Is that the so-called sixth sense, the empathy people can feel for one another when they achieve communication beyond the blind Malkuthian chud that holds us down?

Why did it take the notion of universal destruction to get me to wake up to the only sincere and *vaguely* meaningful relationship in which I dwell?

Maybe I should start answering these questions.

I should start a group that infiltrates the public and threatens them with death. We could call it... Church. But we'd be a lot more subtle about it, and we'd have way more fun. I'm sure we could get the CIA to burn our building down or assassinate me in a matter of months. In this violent political climate a dark horse like myself could come from nowhere and cause a *huge* upset.

Five days isn't much time to organize a world coup. I should have thought of it sooner, but the idea betrays itself, doesn't it?

Do I sound anxious?

Bea didn't come home last night. I waited up for her, and I'm still awake. She normally comes home by seven from an afternoon shift, so by nine I knew she was avoiding me. I thought of calling the restaurant, but I decided against it.

Normally, after a fight like that, I'd be desperate to have her back, to make sure that everything's okay. Last night I felt really satisfied being alone, though. I spent another hour with the picture I had started. I sketched out my design for the picture's background, and I felt like I actually accomplished something. Imagine that.

I've been thinking about the past two days, about how I've been living life, how I reacted to my knowledge of the immanent end. What the... visitor – yeah, the sexless thing with the tail – said to me yesterday:

"God made you free in his image," it said.

That makes sense, somehow. I've *never* been very religious in any serious way. I've spent most of my time being bitter. But, as I'm faced with the inevitable conclusion of *everything*, you can see how I could suddenly become, eh, more *fanatical* than usual, more prone to metaphysical surrender.

I've been a somnambulist for as long as I can remember, sleeping away the hours in a chemical, sexual, low-plane stupor. Now I can't seem to sleep. I'm wide awake. I've been up all night, in fact, *just thinking*.

About an hour ago I moved around to make some breakfast. Our apartment looks pretty good, and with all the dishes cleaned I was able to make myself something nice: chicken fetus and toast and dead pig. I devoured my meal.

These past few days have been one large mood

swing of cosmic proportions. I've never been happier. Why? If the end is near, should I feel joy? I can't help but feel I've misinterpreted the message.

What had Be'ezlebub said? *"The word 'apocalypse' originally meant a revelation."* If not the end, what's being revealed to me?

I want to see the sun rise today. It's really too bad that Bea didn't come home last night, because now I want to share as much time with her as possible. I feel like the light she – the Star of she – gave me in my dream might be just enough to get us across the black gulf and toward one another, the real one another. She'll be happy to know I'm painting again. I wonder what she'll think of my hair, as in my lack of.

I go out to the deck again and watch the sun rise, having watched it set the night before. What a strange thing. The dawn is absolutely golden. There's no other word to describe the color. The leaden blackness of night is made into the purest gold by the sun's energy. Even the polluted air over the city can't deaden the sight of that spectacle. I can't remember the last time I really watched a sunrise.

I watch the sun until after six o'clock. Part of me feels pain that Bea hasn't come home. A moment of panic occurs, because I know she's been out with somebody talking about how crazy her boyfriend is. Hopefully that somebody's a woman. I have no problem with Bea sleeping at a woman's place if we fight, but it's different if she stays with another guy. She can *sleep* with a woman and – for whatever biological, psychological reason – I don't care, but if she so much as stays at a guy's place, I start to get jealous. Or I used to. I've never felt the way I feel now. All I can think about is her *safety*. I want to be pissed, but I know there's no *point* to it. When the anger rises I feel it come into my chest, a sensation very familiar... but now I just breath and let it out, let it go. I close my eyes and can see the light from my dream, green and good.

Am I losing it? If so, then I should lose "it" more often, because I feel fucking fantastic. Looking back over the first day or two of this thing, this makeshift record, and I feel like I've lost the continuity. I don't know what I believe or what's going to happen when the end comes. Maybe it *will* feeling like I'm being squashed by a great, spacious ass – maybe I'll enjoy it as it happens. Maybe it'll be better than sex. Maybe it won't happen at all. I just can't be sure. It changes from moment to moment.

I think about going to bed, but I realize that it would be pointless. I feel too alive, too full of energy. I've gone to a place I *know* nobody else has been.

"You're like the moon. You have four faces. You never show them."

Whispering in my ear again is an echo of my seventh-day-dream. It urges me to behave in a way I've never before considered, to behave in a way contrary to every instinctive fiber inside me. My brain sticks its ass in the air like a porn-star on a trampoline. I'm turned upside down, hung like a horse – no, that's not right. *Hanged* like a horse-thief. That's what I meant to say. Anyway, my world-view has changed.

What way have I been urged to behave? In a *responsible* way. I'm responsible for the light I hold inside me. I'm responsible for my own actions. Ridiculous, I know – counterintuitive, an ugly proposition... to have to care, to be *attached*, to be warm rather than cold.

A lot of lyrics from a lot of songs are swimming in my head, and I'm swimming in them, in return. I think I have some further insight, now. I'm delighted.

The apartment starts to feel small. I kick my legs out on the couch and lay back, blasted and as confused as ever, but with happiness to bolster me. I feel panic again, then annoyed. What kind of a cruel joke is being played on me, to come to these feelings with less than five full days to express them, to *adjust* to them? It's like crushing a butterfly moments before it comes out of the cocoon. *Sick*.

There's a spider on the floor. I step on it,

enjoying the maliciousness of the act. Divine retribution. The good old me, out again, a werewolf in disguise.

Now I feel disgusted with myself. Never before have I been so uncomfortable in my own body. Up and down I go, feeling sublime and aware, then suddenly pained beyond comprehension by the limitations of the awareness, like I'm jumping from the top bunk and hitting my head over and over again on the ceiling.

I'm responsible for my actions.

Ouch.

But then I have absolute freedom. That's not so bad. Of course, I have to *pay* for my actions.

Ouch.

But then I also receive rewards. Right and wrong is relative, isn't it? But I *know* what's wrong because I feel guilty.

Ouch.

Oh, so much choice. What are we going to do with all the choice that we have? What are we going to make of ourselves, you and I, this generation, even with so few days to live. What can be achieved in a couple of days?

This is the right time to become a vegetarian, join a cult, join the military, vote Republican, embrace neo-pagan religion, divine the signs in tea leaves, pick up a Go board, invest in stocks, buy, sell, read everything you can get your hands on, embrace change, accept Jesus as your savior, join the Church of Satan, take ecstacy, heroin, mushrooms, smoke marijuana and opium until your eyes bulge in revelation, drink yourself silly, sleep with a member of the same sex... twice, enjoy a good meal with an old friend, watch a horrible movie and make fun of it, become modern, become post-modern, listen to your *favorite* record... Do anything.

"Do something *now*."
These are the lyrics of a lifetime.
The Question:
Why now?
The Answer:
Why not *now?*

Now's the right time. Because now is no other time but now. Now is now. Now gets to be whenever it wants to be, like a great galactic hippy-vision, like you in your own head, like the beautiful woman across the street who doesn't know she's beautiful, like gurus everywhere who don't know they're gurus yet, like lonely young men who work in gas-stations and can't keep themselves from falling into paranoia, fear – who know not only *that* the world's going to end, but *when* it's going to end, like eye-contact between loved ones, and like *me*. Now gets to be whatever it wants to be.

There are two ways for me to look at time:

1. Between any moment X and any moment Z, there is moment Y.

2. All moments are Y.

These are two viewpoints, both equally true. The first is useful for banking, the second is useful for lovemaking.

Y is a useful shape to express this conception because of the way it looks. It comes from two separate places at the top and unites into one thing at the bottom.

Om. Om. Om.

The great mouth-opening and mouth-closing of universal-big-gang-bang-style sex, cosmic sex, gracious sex, sex-that-is-and-is-not-rape, sex that is more than sex: Adam and Eve style stuff, with leaves and morbid fears *and* innocence – as much as possible of all this and *more*!

Like anything else, this will mislead you if you let it. I've seen enough of life to know that change doesn't come instantaneously like an angel with wings to leap out of a jukebox and jam out for you on its divine harmonica. No, change takes a lot of work.

I want to step into the end feeling like I have a grasp of where I've been. That way, wherever I'm going won't be so bad. If worst comes to worst, I can always dwell comfortably in my memories. That'll be the day, won't it?

In a cultist's dream, we're standing beneath a giant, screaming ziggurat – it screams for attention, it's so large. We're looking at its six stories, but it doesn't have a peak. That annoys the both of us, and we wonder aloud to one another.

Why is the peak missing? What's the point in climbing the gasping, steep tower if there isn't a peak?

Of course it's illogical – wouldn't the top layer be the peak? But six stories don't satisfy us, no, definitely not. We instinctively *know there has to be more and we need that final terrace to satisfy our carnal needs. To our right is a tree with a snake in it.*

We're in the *garden, after all.*

"Oh shit," we think, collectively, for here in this place we are one and so our thoughts are the same. I know yours as you know mine, and we react accordingly. There is very little speech, for it isn't necessary. We've been in this moment before, forever. Now.

The snake sneaks over to you as I go to take a piss. I know you want me to leave you, know you want the snake as near to you as it can get. While I'm gone it whispers something into your ear, and suddenly you've taken a much stronger interest in the way the tree looks.

The tree has five different kinds of fruit on it, fruit – which is odd, for a tree – of five different colors.

And now you offer me a cherry. I know where it has come from. I know the story, so I try... I try really hard not to eat the red fruit. But because my will is yours, and you want only the best for me... you want me to eat. So I eat.

As I take the first bite, my eyes dart, moved by some unseen mover. That's a whale of an idea, really... an unseen mover! – upward and toward the great architecture beneath which we stand, the huge ziggurat that left us so dissatisfied.

Now, finally, there's a seventh step and an appropriate top to the pyramid. The snake disappear with the garden as our paradise fades, and we're thrust onto the first step, blind and naked and unsure. From our place the ziggurat everything in our view has changed, and we don't see the top. We can't even see the next level. It takes a very short amount of time for us to realize that we're naked, and in our embarrassment we forget about where we are.

We forget about there ever being a seventh level, a snake, and a cherry. That's myth *now.*

Spice, cook for 50,000 years, and eventually people put one another in complex incinerators and drop nuclear bombs on one another, crash planes into buildings. What's worst, while people do these terrible things, they talk all the goddamned while.

It's a beautiful tapestry to watch, sure, but to be a part of it doesn't always feel that good. It feels terrible, in fact. I'm not sure I *like* to consider myself a human. Then what am I? Where's our promised divinity, the god-in-us? Has it disappeared, or are we only neglecting it for the benefit of the economy?

Bombs=$.

Is there any wonder people distract themselves in the most fundamentally ridiculous ways? I know I do.

Girls are beautiful. Aren't they just? That's a bomb.

In my mind's eye I see a tall woman with graceful movements and wonderfully long legs, a face that I should frame, and eyes that glow. I see every tiny blond hair on her face. They run up and around her lips, thin and faint, just white enough to create a shimmering halo around her cheeks. Her eyes are green. I sink into their eyes, and suddenly it's the seventh day once again, and I'm floating around in a green world. It doesn't take long for my vision of that woman to become a vision of Bea, and Bea to become that woman. I wonder.

Is this "fundamentally ridiculous"? Does being "verbose" mean that you use so many complicated words that you stab yourself in the gut with hypocritical turn-arounds and mistreated phrases?

I hope so. I sure do. I want contradiction, more than anything I want contradiction. I don't want anybody to be able to understand what I'm saying unless they're able to accept contradiction. Contradiction is ineffable, paradox is divine, oneness is fraudulent, unpredictable, majestic. I want that. I want *her*, the one whose veil won't be lifted.

Bea is beautiful. Bea's been there before, in that garden I described beneath the ziggurat. She understands something of the snake, something I'll never – not in this life as a male – understand, something I can never hope to grasp. It works both ways, though, which means *I* must know something that she doesn't. It empowers, that idea.

Be'elzebub was there somewhere, too. If it can get into my apartment, what would keep it out of a *garden*, for Christ's sake? Or a desert? Not a whole lot, I'm sure. I think it can be whatever it wants. Everything we see is just reflecting light back to us, so it should be easy for an ally of *"he who gives light"* to take whatever form suits it.

I stand up and grab my painting supplies. I glance over my shoulder at the bedroom and the place where the creature had stood yesterday. I'm fumbling with my keys as I lock the door, suddenly nervous that I might have to see it again. It told me what I needed to hear... in a way.. but overall, the experience was creepy.

I step out of the building and walk with my supplies and the sketch toward a nearby park. The sun on my back energizes me. It feels great.

I'm not normally up at eight in the morning. I forgot how great the morning air smells, how it fills up the lungs and makes everything seem different. Life's lighter in the morning air.

When I get to the park I set up my supplies: my small stand, the paints, the sketch, everything I brought with. I sit beneath the tree and paint. I use the tree as the background for the painting. I try to set Be'ezlebub beneath the tree which, in turn, is beneath the ziggurat of my dream. It seems appropriate, but I'm not sure *why*. Its tail looks like the snake should, the way I paint.

To my far right is a pagoda. I'm so busy in my paints that I don't notice a small jazz band set up. People file in through all around the neighborhood – the park is near a lake, and in the summer people go swimming, canoe, eat ice-cream – and settle down to listen to the band. The band tunes, then plays.

I, in the meantime, pull the appropriate colors out of my palette: greys and blacks for Be'elzebub, greens and reds for the tree and cherries: earth tones for the ziggurat. I spend hours painting.

At one point, closer to the noon than the

morning, a girl – maybe ten years old; I'm not very good at gauging age – walks up to me. She stands over my shoulder and asks, "What are you painting? He looks *familiar*."

Eerie. I look back at her and smile a little. She has red juice stains around her small lips. Ehm... "Who?" I glance around.

She points at the painting, toward the creature with the tail. "Him."

I blink, realizing who she's talking about. Good creeping Jesus, that's weird. "I'm sure you don't know him," I say quickly.

She shrugs and stares at me, looks into my eyes calmly. I turn back to my painting and keep working. The band has stopped and another group has taken their place. Apparently there's a blues festival this week that started today.

"Angel," I hear a woman's voice call. "Anjel, honey, come here." There's only the slightest difference in the enunciation between the word "Angel" and the girl's name. I'm not even sure if that's her name, but it seems like the right thing to write down. It could be both, or either, or *neither*. The mother says it in a very familiar way, though, which leads me to think it might be her name.

"I have to go," the girls says, sparkly. "It's a pretty painting."

[T-] 100

I glance back at her. When I turn around, she's running to her mother. Next to her mother, just over the woman's left shoulder, stands Be'elzebub. It has a light in its eyes, bright and wide, that seems to say everything and nothing.

I understand, and I don't. It works, though, to feel the ambiguity.

It disappears, a blink-flash of light, then lightlessness.

As I put the finishing touches on the first day's work and step away, I stop long enough at the pagoda to throw five dollars down for the musicians. I listen to an alto saxophone solo – a small white guy wails until he breaks a sweat, then falls back amidst the rest of the band – and then a forty-year-old black trumpeter steps up. He spits blast after blast of sound from his instrument. His face glows under the sun until he descends into silent depths, steps away from the front of the stage, then relaxes back into his chair under the pagoda's polite shade, free from the glaring, self-evident sunlight.

The world is going to end in four days, and what follows will be my record, the recording of my experience of the spacious, *infinite* macrocosm's conclusion

Maybe somebody will have a chance to read it before the end. Maybe I'll post it to the net, somebody will get it before the world ends and will be inspired – not that it matters. They won't even be able to read the last moments, if what I say is true, unless I set up some kind of live-on-the-spot writing... in a chat room or something.

Why bother?

Why not *bother?*

Oh Internet – society's new least common denominator, like an incredibly powerful and mostly interactive public radio. *Anybody* can say most *whatever* they want, whenever they want, in whatever language they want, and can expect to have *some* kind of an audience, and why shouldn't we?

The worst thing a person can expect from misuse of the net is a loss of vague social status and maybe a bit of self-esteem, but because the average person doesn't *have* any – that is, status or self-esteem – to begin with, most people don't have much to lose, and besides, on the net you can always use a pseudonym. So computerization provides the outlet which lowers absolutely the least common denominator – people do, can, and will say things online they'd never consider saying elsewhere in public.

It isn't very difficult anymore to get your words heard, no matter how ridiculous, inane, or even worthless they are. Most people have even lost the belief in worthlessness. *Everything*, in this culture, has value, because even if something – a painting, an idea, a *coin* – *doesn't*, there will always be somebody out there to lie and say that it *does,* to maintain the cultural continuity, the snowball effect of value-inflation.

We *fear* to declare anything worthless, because in doing so we might betray our own feelings of worthlessness, inadequacy, and all the rest. So everybody has a place to shout out – and it's a good thing, too. It might make the collective unconscious more apparent. Can't hurt.

People squawk a lot about privacy today, and I think a lot of it has to do with a recently increased anonymity that interconnected computers allow people to achieve . The web *preserves* anonymity as much as it allows another to encroach upon privacy. The threats to privacy come when the *new* anonymity is threatened, but the threats weren't there before. Like any technology, the Internet is a double-edged blade, and when it's whipped out and flashed, there's a risk having it used against us return.

We can say most anything – for instance – under the shroud of general technological anonymity. Likewise, a savvy hacker can access most *anything* digital that's connected to the Internet. Think about it. *Anything*. All the files. Secrets piled upon secrets, and if a person's smart enough... a back stage pass to your behavior patterns is a couple of keystrokes away.

Go online and see what you can find about the end of the world. You think I'm the only person who thinks, knows, believes beyond a doubt, that the world's going to end? Open your eyes and ears to the least common digital denominator. Experience the waves beneath the popular press and media, then enjoy the insanity you see and hear. There are a thousand groups, a million individuals who suffer – enjoy? – end of the world paranoia, delusions, and conspiratorial floundering. *I am not alone*. And if you believe me, neither are you.

Enjoy the way that we can access the collective unconscious with a point and a click or a turn of a dial. It's pretty incredible. They say that information is free, and in a pretty big way it is. But *should* it be? We have just as much access to terrible, insane ideas as we have access to sublime, wonderful ideas. Of course, who decides the qualities of an idea?

[T-] 105

Trippy. Data. Delicious, fluid, surreal and sublime information. Inconceivably large, the bytes and bytes and bytes – all those 1s and 0s hurt my head. + and - making words and numbers and ideas that span the planet, linked by cord and satellite. More words, more images than one person could possibly read or view in an entire lifetime, in a thousand lifetimes. Hours and hours of scrolling and you'd never even chip into the surface of what's there to find, true or untrue, pleasing or ugly, real or *surreal*.

The sheer volume that exists is a testament to the reality of a collective human experience.

So experience as much as you can as often as possible – this can be a new medieval millenium's motto, a new creed for the confused crack-children... the children stuck in the valley, the children who slipped in between, let themselves slip, decided to slip, wanted to be *that special way* with *that special look* in all three of their eyes.

Judge not, we've been taught. But to be initiated into anything – work, school, higher knowledge – judgement *must* occur.

I think we *should* judge. I think we should judge as much as possible, so often so that we ourselves *will* be judged and *will* be forced onto that proverbial cross. That way this generations martyrdom won't be voluntary.

If your martyrdom is voluntary, you're committing suicide. And suicide is boring. It's been done before, like a rerun of the infinite sitcom. Suicide is your opinions – your judgement – turned in on yourself. Project them outward. Enjoy the taste of vile, black spittle running down your lips as you yell at the driver in the next lane who cut you off. He's probably from some state – state of mind, I mean – you'll never visit. So don't worry. Yell.

It's dark in our apartment. The television is on. I haven't bothered to watch television in a long time, but right now, at four in the morning, *these are my people*.

"Children of the Lord!" a man in a blond wig bellows across the waves of space-time, a golden Bible in his hands. Who knows if he's recording this right now or this is a canned "episode"? I don't. I don't even know if *he* knows, and there's no way for me to call him and ask. He is, to me, a stranger.

He stands in front of a disgusting-looking blue-screen which shows a not-very-imaginative vision of Hell. It doesn't look like I think Hell should. It looks like the interior of somebody's furnace, not the highly-lighted Sartrerian conception of Hell that I have. I think about personal hells, not the Hell of fire and brimstone. I think of *Sisyphus*, of Killing an Arab.

"Children of the Lord," he repeats, as if we didn't hear him the first time. "Surely the Signs are appearing."

A picture of the Twin Towers bops up on the screen, followed by the familiar mushroom cloud of an atomic explosion, followed by an image of some rock star in drag who holds a golden Bible of his own, followed finally by an image of the four horsemen of the apocalypse, horribly drawn red riders wielding archaic weapons of war.

"Surely, the Signs are upon us," he whispers now. Beads of sweat drip down his greasy forehead, splash dangerously onto his golden Book.

"And what does *The BOOK* have to say about these times?! Revelation chapter 4, verse 1... 'Then as I looked, I saw a door standing open in heaven, and the same voice I had heard before, that sounded like a might trumpet blast, spoke to me and said, 'Come up here and I will show you what must happen in the future!' And truly that future is *NOW*!" he screams. A poorly recorded sound of a trumpet blowing accompanies an fiery image of Satan on the weird man's blue-screen.

I laugh. I think about my new friend with the tail. What would it think? I imagine it'd say, "The signs have always been upon you. Oh, and Satan doesn't look like that. He comes as a gentleman, and he always orders dessert when you're paying the bill, and he always fucks you up the ass when you're not looking, and he's *glad* you're an avaricious, greedy bastard, he's glad you're wearing the $ armband. He's quite glad."

Is it dangerous to put words into a demon's mouth? What does that say about my psyche, when my new favorite fantasy involves some androgynous demon with a glowing tail? Should I throw out my comic books – pardon me, my "graphic novels" – and seek therapy, or should I proceed with life as always?

Should I think about my childhood?

I'm in fourth grade. The room is perfectly square. I don't know why, but there's no teacher present. This is Hell. I feel strange, small, underdeveloped. Is that a feeling you can have: underdeveloped? I think so, because that's how I feel.

I'm putting words I didn't know then to the situation, which is strange. It's strange to travel time and describe things in a way you never knew you felt, even though you lived through the things you describe.

Anyway, we're in the process of showing our art to one another, and I'm the only person in front of the room. Suddenly there's a wet feeling, and everybody laughs.

Good Goddamned Lord, I've wet *myself!*

Ha ha. Hee hee. Ha ha. Young people squeal, snort, make noises that are far uglier to me than the mistake I've made.

[T-] 109

I rationalize all these things away. We all do. And if you haven't, you aren't human as I know it... or you know something I don't, maybe *the* secret.

Maybe you were the kid that the adults chose to be a symbol, that Nazi-poster child, used and discarded, sent away early and made into something you never wanted to be, something through which other people live vicariously... like an imaginary devil at the foot of middle-aged-peoples' beds, smiling at them in the dark.

"He's a good boy. He's smart. He'll go far. He'll do great things. He'll make something of himself."

"That's odd. I always thought he would fuck up."

Chatter chatter chatter chatter, voices and more voices, a fiery inferno of cackle – obsessively loud. Can you hear them when you put your head down on your pillow? Are you connected? Or are you in an urn somewhere below the ground, no better than an expensive ash-tray for your biological machine's remains? When do we die? If we stop living before the end comes, are we already dead. Does the technical definition we have of death – of the stoppage of brain activity, of bodily death – keep us from realizing we can die long before our bodies do?

I think so.

We're all ground up beneath somebody else's wheel, which is a pretty astounding *revelation* when you

[T-] 110

first realize it. Somebody else is above who you're below, and above *everything* is the wheel of the Æons. It grinds us all to a pulp, with time, doesn't it? It will. It has. It will forever.

We humans can't help but replicate the process. We're a part of it. Most of our institutions are spokes on our great social wheel. The spoke that is modern public education consists of Institutes for the Unharmonious Development of Man.

"Hey, teacher... throw them kids a bone!"

Where is the teacher now?

I think of a whale... being in the belly of it. I'm ready to be devoured by its infernal acids. This whale is – for a great many of us – school, it is *education*, it is *society*:

"*that in which we live, move, and have our being.*"

And the other children are laughing. Of course they're laughing. I'd laugh.

These are the moments that formed me, the moments that still knot me stomach into a ball whenever I pick up a pen or a paintbrush or go to a job interview. I don't know why, but I never really gotten over *something*.

And I'm not alone in that.

What could it be? What is it that we haven't gotten over?

You spend years on a therapists couch or years smoking dope... maybe you spend years smoking dope on a couch... and you never quite know why you can't sit comfortably by yourself, until finally somebody offers a fast solution and you're prey to something like the guy on the television with the blue screen behind him.

Blind yourself so you'll be led around more easily, but be prepared to suffer the consequences when you're given the purple drink from the barrel or are asked to perform terrible rituals of sodomy in front of the fat-man's digital camera. Your reputation will be ruined, and you'll forever be that President who got his cock sucked beneath the desk, that person nobody else can really touch or love or know. You'll be that puppet painted black.

Is that what you really want to be?

Those children still laugh at me when I let them.

There are four things I dread: fear, anger, loneliness, and your judgement. I think about the four riders of the Apocalypse and the four days we all have left to live. At least I'm on top now: I know. I've achieved gnosis, knowledge... of something, at least, even if it's the ultimate minus sign, the final negation, [T-] four days.

There will be no more X's or Y's or Z's or embarrassing moments to keep you or me down, not

[T-] 112

after this Saturday. There'll be no more awkward moments at parties and shows when you don't know what to say or how to approach that one, beautiful guy or girl without seeming like a freak. There will be no more addictions or codependencies or rent checks or gods or devils...

There won't be anything at all.

Or maybe... or maybe something... new... more *terrifying*.

In social situations the Shadow threatens to bubble up at any given moment. One drink too many and suddenly you're stepping into the forest, ready to do battle with your friend Enkidu against the terrible Humbaba that you *know* you are. Of course, it's rare to find Enkidu safe and sound inside of you – rare, because most of us have had the potential for it beaten out of us: Dionysus, Bacchus, Osiris... Buddha-consciousness, Christ-consciousness, or the higher guardian angel, *whatever*. These ideas are not compatible with the modern, social, overly-garrulous demands of human life. People don't want you to bring Humbaba out of your pocket. He's supposed to be safe in the forest, hidden from view. As soon as you bring your friend Enkidu to the party, they know you're heading toward the smell of pines, and they don't want to be near you anymore. They want to stay safe and sound in the lowlands. No danger. No risk. No surprises.

Everyone wants to be a lazy king or a lazy queen, wants to be Gilgamesh without the burden of the forest.

"You have four faces," she said. "You never show them."

I know the four things I *dread*. What would their opposites be? Would those be goals to achieve, aims to shoot for, ways toward which to evolve? Yes.

Fear... Courage.

Anger... Calm.

Loneliness... Togetherness.

Judgement... Acceptance.

The four things I seek: courage, calm, togetherness, and acceptance.

Those are my four faces, the four I never show.

Are those my four faces, the four I never show?

I see myself beneath that tree with the thin monk and the fat monk, but the tree isn't changing. My hands are wide. I offer something up. The monks are strong from my offering, no longer thin or fat, but they're right in between. They both smile. Their bowls are full. The tree doesn't grow, neither does it shed leaves. It is stopped. It is *summer*, the fulfilled.

My painting turned out better than I thought it would, and why shouldn't it have? For the first time in my life I have a true muse, a real vision to share. It isn't really a regular still-life, but I think with the right frame it might pass as a professional effort.

Bea will bea the final judge. Ha ha ha.

"Ahem."

Like clockwork – just when I think of her, which is a nice synchronicity – she unlocks the door. It opens, and she steps through. She looks tired but good. Her eyes go wide as she steps into the apartment. She notices me immediately, all my glorious mop gone. As she tosses her backpack down, she says "What happened to your hair?" I can tell she's making an effort to be calm.

"I cut it off."

"And who cleaned the apartment?" she asks. She looks me in the eye, her own narrow. They betray anger, "You had somebody else over, didn't you?" She approaches me, baring her teeth. "One day, it took. You bastard."

I shrug and say, "You might say that. I'm not sure. It wasn't really much of a person. It had a glowing tail."

She steps back. She's wearing the same clothes that she left with, and they're a little ruffled. She probably slept in them. "What do you mean by *that*?" she asks. "And aren't you usually in bed by four?"

I hold my hands up defensively. She stops, stares,

and before I can answer her questions, asks, "What happened to your hands?" She steps forward and grabs one of them, holding my fingers in hers. My hands are covered with red paint, sticky, from when I touched up the cherries in the painting. A moment passes, and she pulls away, not ready yet to be comfortable with me.

I turn my hands over and look at them. "It's just paint," I laugh.

"Paint?" she asks, showing her teeth in a half-smile. "You were painting?"

"Yeah. Come and see." I stand up from the couch and show her the canvas. She steps toward it and looks closely.

"That's pretty good." She glances over at me, then points toward the subject. "Who's that?"

"That's a really long story. It's the thing that was... here," I say, clearing my throat. I go into the kitchen and wash my hands with soap, ridding my palms and digits of the redness. I come back and put my hand around her waist. She freezes momentarily, then I feel her tension melt. I say, "I hope you haven't been with anybody *I* don't know,"

"I was *trying* to avoid you. I didn't think you'd be up now, so I came home."

"Where were you going to go if not stay here?" I ask. I look down at her face over her shoulder. We make eye contact.

She shrugs and leans a little bit back into me. "This painting is pretty good. I didn't know you were going to start again." She moves forward, pushing away from me, then turns around challengingly, "You've been acting really fucked-up lately. What's wrong with you?"

"It's a long story," I exhale – piteously, I'm sure.

"I have the time." I laugh... It's not appropriate, but I laugh. She thinks I'm laughing at her. "What's so funny?"

I slide back onto the couch and place my head on the cushions. Through my laughter, which sounds, even to me, manic and desperate, I reply, "I'm just not sure you really have the time."

"That end of the world thing? The Apocalypse thing? The Armageddon thing? That's crazy. I told you before. That's fucking *crazy*! I told Shelly about that – I was at her place – and she thinks I need to call a hospital or something. I talked to Blake. If it hadn't been for him, I wouldn't have even *bothered* coming back."

Blake is an old friend – one of my oldest. We'd slept with him some months back and hadn't seen him around much since. Suddenly I feel sad I hadn't kept in touch. "That's nice of him," I mutter.

"Just... explain this to me."

"If I tell you something – a lot of something, something that might sound insane at first – will you just please *listen?*"

She blinks, stares at me. "I'm not even sure I know who you are anymore. We haven't talked in months. I'm not sure if we've *ever* really talked, because I don't feel like I know you." She looks like she might start crying. I'm impressed with her. She looks, in the soft light of our apartment, the sun threatening to dawn shortly, like she did in my dream.

I take a deep breath, then exhale. I let it all out in a rapid blast of explanation, of exposition.

I talk to her as if she's the Star of herself.

I tell her about my vision at the gas station, about

July 27th at 6:10 p.m.

about my feelings, our relationship, and my anxiety. I tell her about my vision on the seventh day, about the demonic visitation on the fifth day. I pull out some of my notes and tell her my feelings.

She laughs and stares, fumes and thinks, but best of all, she really listens.

"And that's who you painted? That thing? It was in our room?" she asks, after she's listened for nearly an hour to my chatter.

"Yeah. It's incredible." I pause, then ask the fundamental question. "Do you think I'm crazy?"

"I don't think you need to touch any drugs

anymore... ever," she says. She looks estranged, unlike the Bea I've grown used to, like we're getting to know one another for the first time again.

Maybe we never really knew one another at all.

She reaches out a hand and puts it on my head, strokes the little fuzz growing out of my scalp. "I don't think you're really crazy, *but* I don't think the world's going to end either. It's important that you tell me about all your imaginary friends from now on. That way I'll know who you're talking to when you start muttering to yourself."

She thinks this is *funny*.

I nod. I don't want to get into a debate over the reality of these visions. Who's to say what's real?

"Will you spend the next few days with me?" I ask.

"Yeah," she says, moving closer to me on the couch. "I wasn't sure what I was going to do. I thought I might leave. I still don't know. I don't understand what's happened to you."

"I feel like I'm alive again. It's so *odd*, to think the world's coming to an end, then to reach this point where I feel *aware* and more conscious than ever."

"You seem happier," she says, half-smiling. "Do you want to know how *I've* been?" she asks.

"Sure," I reply.

"I've been *pissed*," she says, though her voice is soft. "You pissed me off! You know I've never been with a guy as long as I've been with you, and now you've gone off the deep end," she says. "It's like... 'Great, Bea... you're with an absolute psycho. Typical.'"

Clearly she doesn't know how she feels, really, about my sanity. I'll let the idea settle before I argue further.

She'll understand in three days, or I'll be proven wrong and everything will go on as it has... except for me. I'll be changed. I am changed.

She pauses, then rubs her stomach a little, "And I've felt a little sick lately. I've thrown up a few times."

I reach out and pet her hair. "Ohh... I'm sorry. You should let me take care of you." I frown a little, and after a short silence add, "It's your choice who you're with, you know."

"That dream you had sounded beautiful. I wonder where it came from," she says, ignoring the plea inherent in my suggestion.

"So do I."

The day has begun to break, but rainclouds block the sun. The first hard drops of rain hit our basement window. I love that sound. It's like the rain can hold you, comfort you, keep you indoors and force you to face your domestic life. When the gods weep for joy, we get rain.

[T-] 120

I'm almost weeping for joy, myself. I'm glad she's here. "I want you to be with me until this thing happens, until the moment comes."

"Why?"

"Because I want us to be together."

She smiles, kisses me on the lips, backs away. "I think I like you this way. We should join an apocalypse cult. We could drink some Kool-Aid together. It would be more romantic than the last year together."

I give her a hard look, which she easily breaks with a laugh. I'm not really offended. It's just... I still believe that it's going to end. "You'll be here, though, right?"

"Sure, yeah. I don't have to work Saturday."

"Do you work today?"

"Nooooo...." she says, and she's dipping her hand down my cherry-covered boxers – all I'm wearing. The rain splatters outside as she takes me out, plays with me, leans over.

I push my head back again and smile. "If we came in with a bang, we might as well go out with one," I mumble.

She rolls her eyes up to me, leans up, keeps her hand on me... "You really think the way the end's going to feel is like me sitting on your face?"

"Yup." I lean in to kiss her. "Or maybe like this."

We kiss for a while before she says, "Y'know,"

through a kiss. She breaks off to say, "I want to be there when you think it's going to end, just so I can laugh when you're wrong. You're going to have to get another job. You're going to have to admit that you're *wrong*. You think you can do that? It'll make you more like everybody else, for you to *apologize*. It'll be good for you."

"I thought I might paint..."

She squints, stops moving her hand in that o-so-beautiful way... claws the tip of my cock slightly. "Jesus!" I shout. "Okay, I'll get a job again, and I'll admit that I was wrong... If it doesn't happen. *If!*"

"Damned right," she snorts, then goes back to the nice stuff. "Our friends all want to know where you've been."

"I don't want to see anybody except you." That's the first time in a year of knowing her that I've said that. She looks at me, a light of recognition in her eyes. Strange, that it comes so naturally... now. "You're beautiful, Bea." She squints her eyes a little. I've said things *similar* to these before, but something's different this time. I feel a glow when I talk to her. I knew it would be different. I'm just glad that she came back.

"Thanks."

Mere minutes pass before we're in the throws of passionate foreplay, and for the first time in a month we make sober love without speaking to one another – good love, total connection, absolute adoration... spirit love, sublime yoni and divine lingam. The rain stops, and we fall asleep in one another's arms, exhausted and aglow.

That day there's a flash flood warning for many parts along the Mississippi, including Minneapolis and St. Paul. We sleep through the day, having found higher ground... in our basement apartment.

Thrice Calls Amore'
3 Days
Morning

Beeeeeeeeeeeeeeeeeeeeeeeeeeeeee
                eeeeeeeeeeeeeeeeeeeeeeeeeeee
                                eeeeeeeeeeeeeeeeeee
p

It's almost eleven in the morning. I'm still exhausted, despite having had almost ten hours of sleep. I can still feel the wine we drank last night – after the sex – course through my system.

"I have to go to work, but I'll come right home afterwards," she had said a half an hour ago. I believe her. I know she'll be back home this time.

I roll over and let the wine take me away.

The curtain opens.

A dozen children stand on a small stage, dressed in tin-foil and green wrapper. They look like little blobs of quickly completed art-projects, and if they were adults it would be shameful... artistically shameful, socially damaging, and mentally questionable. As children, it only looks childish. *These are pre-schoolers. They don't yet have to worry about what they wear. Their parents are responsible.*

One of them, a young Japanese boy with thick black hair, walks up to a microphone on the left. He wears a big white hat and has a white tail that drags a few feet behind him. It's made out of dish-cloths.

Somebody evil plays a few notes on a piano, poorly.

"I am a sp-ew-em," the Japanese boy says into the microphone. He leans too closely to the microphone, and a broad crackle accompanies his tensely memorized line. The audience grows tense, and an awkward rush blows over them. Everybody pretends not to notice it or be annoyed, but the undercurrent is hideous.

Will this thing hold, Mrs. Paterson wonders, or will the parents come to her later with a rake and a chainsaw and demand retribution.

She could have her license revoked, would be forced back into substitute teaching... high school gym classes.

Noooooo!

A little blond girl with pigtails approaches a microphone on the other side of the stage. The evil force on the piano bangs out a few more chords.

"I am an egg," the girl enunciates, precise but unsteady. She keeps herself too far away from the microphone, so she's difficult to hear, but at least she said the line correctly.

Mrs. Patterson breathes a sigh of relief and goes back to fingering herself behind stage.

The curtain drops. Everybody claps. When the curtain re-opens, there's a plastic baby in the middle of the stage. Above it is a glowing pyramid with an eye in the center.

"The medieval alchemists used code-language to describe the process of revelation and eventual transcendence. Through the proverbial alkhemical *wedding the universal* panacea *can,* these thinkers posited, be discovered: the device by which all questions are resolved, and lead is turned into gold. The process involved sacred psychology, sacred sexuality, as well as an understanding of the heavenly elements and their symbolic meaning," a tall young man with a shaved head says.

All the pre-school children nod sagely. They look ridiculous in their costumes. The sperm and the egg sit next to one another on stage. The sperm tries to kiss the egg, who pushes the sperm away. She blushes and giggles, then looks around to see if anybody else noticed.

"The nature of the cosmic triad is such that there is a positive, a negative, and a reconciling force. All things exists in balance not because it is perfectly matched by its opposite, but because an infinite harmony exists between two polarities, brought together in a fine synthesis through the interference of the third force. The son can not know the father without the intervention of the holy
speeeeeeeeeeeeeeeeeeeeeeeeeeeeeeeeeeeee
eeeeeeeeeeeeeeeeeeeeeeeeeeee
eeeeeeeeeeeeeeeeeee

p

I hit the snooze button and roll over again, this time to my other side. I blink just long enough to notice a ray of sunlight that creeps through a crack in our window. I feel a mild anxiety, but I'm quickly asleep. There's no need to worry. Is there?

I hit the water on my back, but it doesn't sting. The water welcomes me, folds around me, makes my arms wings. It feels nice, soothes... brings the heat of my body down to its level, which is like warm ice. I feel *joyous*.

Somewhere outside of my dream it's still raining, and there's still a flood warning. I sense it, feel it, but it's distant, meaningless compared to the immediate moisture around me.

I kick, send myself in a smooth glide to the surface of the water. I'm in the center of a pyramid. Above me looms a giant eye. Wide open, it stares outward with beams of light that glow, glow, glow, glow... glow...

I tread water for a short while before I tire, then swim to the edge of the pyramid. All around the pyramid's four sides is a ten foot white sandy beech. Here I meet a troupe of three adventurers, a dwarf, an elf, and a halfling. I don't see them until I reach shore.

"Hello, human," the elf says. She's beautiful and has large breasts, long eye-lashes, looks like she was imported from the front cover of a bad fantasy novel. She's nearly naked and holds a long, phallic broadsword.

I want to jump her, mount her, bite the little tips of her elfin ears off... y'know, *make her mine*. "Hello, there," I say. The line doesn't sound appropriate... not with that eye looming over my shoulder.

The dwarf stomps up to me. This thing is male, half my size, twice my width, with the typical red hair and sour attitude.

"This dream isn't up to par with my last ones..." I say, looking down at the cookie-cutter dwarf.

"Aye', 'tis na'eght, but 'as na'eght o'eeeer probleaghm, i'nt, hmm?" He stares at me, then says to the halfling, "Look wha' theaghy deeeed tae 'is cack."

I'm naked. He *apparently* refers to the way I'm cut. Amazing. I'm too busy staring at the elf's cleavage to care what the dwarf thinks about my penis. She's too busy staring at the huge glowing eye that looms omnisciently over the great lake at the pyramid's center to notice my impolite, sexually-charged stare.

The halfling and the dwarf chortle together regarding the size and shape of my package, but I don't mind. They're figments of my imagination, so there's no point letting them bother me.

It would only make things worse, I tell myself.

Instead of dwelling on the truly huge proportions down below, I step to the elf-creature's left, meet her stare, then join her in her gaze at the great gaping eye. It has nice, long lashes, though I don't know whether or not it even has lids. It's difficult to tell because of the bright light which comes from it.

"What is that?" I ask the elf, leaving the halfling and the dwarf to their axes and daggers and dragons.

"That," she says, "is the eye of R'eal, keeper of the sacred places between X and Z and even Y." She pulls a leather pouch out, takes a piece of beef jerky between her teeth and proceeds to eat some. She offers me a piece, which I take and munch. "In other words," she proceeds, "it's the all-seeing-eye-of-what-you-would-probably-call-God."

"Wow," I say, treating the eye with a new kind of a respect. Now I know why I feel so strange. "What's it doing here?"

"Thaegh's aye's gooood a queaghst'on aeght aye've heargh'd... awwwwl daeghy," the dwarf snorts.

"What the fuck is he saying?" I ask the elf.

"I have no idea. I don't even know how I ended up here." She rubs her right arm. "I've got an ink mark on my arm, like somebody's been writing on me – poorly – and I don't know why."

"You're in the wrong place," I say. "I think that's the problem."

"That again?" she says. "That's the fifth time this month. Do you know how many times that happens? It's difficult, being a stereotype." Her heaving breasts move downward slightly as she slumps.

The eye, meanwhile, remains unblinking.

I put an arm on the elf's shoulder. "That's okay. Not everybody can be an elaborately constructed character, deep in substance and literary importance. If it's any consolation, you're part of *my* vision of the eye-of-God."

She rolls her eyes and turns away. I glance back at the halfling and the dwarf. They shrug.

"She's been like this since we got here," the halfling says. "I'm just excited about whatever treasure we're going to find. That eye must guard something pretty amazing. It *never* blinks."

"En' aye'm heyeargh fer' tha' booty," the dwarf says, ridiculously. "Aye'm thaegh son o' God. This heargh is God." He points over to the halfling.

"That's the Holy Spirit," the halfling says. He gestures to the elf.

"I'll bet she's *full* of holy spirit," I say quietly, smirking. The halfling giggles. The dwarf snorts and begins to dig in the dirt.

I walk over to the elf, who chews delicately on her jerky. She has long, beautiful legs, gorgeous blond hair, is muscular, intelligent, and – best of all – looks like she's ready to *breed*: everything for which an up and coming warrior could hope.

And I *am* that up and coming warrior.

Before I can say anything, to prove my worthiness, she interrupts, "Let me guess. You're writing something about the end of the world."

"How'd you know that?" I ask, genuinely taken aback.

"That's the only time I become conscious... when the world's about to end or *might* be about to end, if only some group of heroes can find some item and throw it into some damned mountain, or *whatever*. It's typical. All you people are the same. Whenever you go on a dry spell – you aren't getting laid, whatever – you find the cheapest literary device you can and exploit it. It's sad."

"I don't want to exploit *you*," I lie, pathetically. "You aren't a literary device. This is a *dream*."

It's my dream, though, and aside from the bulging eye of God, there's nothing to alarm me.

I could kick the dwarf across this huge pyramid without blinking. I just know I could. All I'd have to do is *imagine* myself doing so, and it would happen.

The she-elf looks long into my eyes, and we exchange energy, or I *imagine* that we do. "Want to find a tree somewhere?" I ask coyly. I wink, nudge, prod, push, suggest, weasel, and basically flirt my way forward. If all else fails, *flirt*.

The elf shrugs, "Why not? What else am I going to do? I'm your creation, aren't I?"

I glance up at the eye of God. I wonder if he feels jealous...

"I'm your creation," she repeats.

I laugh as we frolic along the beach. The she-elf has her clothes off in moments and we roll around on the sand. "I'm your creeeeeeeeeeeeeeeeeeeeeeeeeeeeeeeee
eeeeeeeeeeeeeeeeeeeeeeeeeeeeeeeeeeee
eeeeeeeeeeeeeeeeeeeeeeeeeee

p.

I have a mouthful of pillow between my teeth. *Damnit!*
Why me?
Just when the dream was starting to make *sense*.

I hit the snooze button for a third time. If I fall asleep quickly enough perhaps I'll return to where I left off.

No such luck.

"How's your vision, light-bearer?" it asks.
"Fine."

"Really? You aren't nervous, or paranoid, or confused? You don't feel like a pasta dish anymore? You feel *good*?" the demon asks me. Blackness looms all around us. In the far distance is a deep, black sun.

A black sun? I'd take the dwarf over enormous celestial anomalies.

"Yeah, I feel good. I've been painting. Nothing much matters to me. It's going to end in two days, all of this. Remember? I had the vision. I'm the one who *knows*."

"You haven't got much of a brain on you, you know that?"

"What's that supposed to mean? You're *in* my brain. You're a figment of my imagination. I'm creating you right now. You're from a part of my subconscious, at best."

"That's a particularly *trite* response. Do you know how many times I've heard that since the sixties?"

It stares at me, as if I should know. I don't give it the benefit of a response.

It goes on, "Anyway, never mind. I'm here to tell you that you're supposed to keep up the good work. You've been doing a fantastic job with your girlfriend. We're actually beginning to believe that you *love* her, and if you can fool us, you can definitely fool her. She's not the brightest brick in the wall."

[T-] 134

"But I *do* love her."

There's a big crash of lightening and immediately Be'ezlebub's face turns from that which I know into something hideous, a spacious maw with a thousand teeth, a tongue like fire, eyes inky and dark. When the lightening fades, Be'ezlebub has returned back to normal, with the cashmere, nice pants, humanoid shape, and the familiar glowing tail. "I'll pretend I didn't hear that," it snarls, its composure gone.

Do I *finally* have the upper hand here? I think so.

I shrug. I'm not afraid. I'm dreaming. It's not like Be'ezlebub is in my room with me. It's in my *head* with me. "I meant what I said, though. I love her. I'm going to tell her that when she comes home. I've never told her that before. I should have said it a *long* time ago." I pause. It looks displeased. I smile. "Have *you* ever loved anybody?"

Lightening, like the flash of a camera, crashes through my head. There is no thunder.

The demon doesn't even have time to sneer at me. The black sun sucks it back inside from whence it came. "Thanks for painting me, you stupid bastard," it yells back to me from the pits of hell. The word "bastard" echoes a few times – *bastard-astard-stard-tard-ard-rd-d* – and then there's silence.

For some reason I don't think I'll have to deal

with *that* again, which is good. After the world ends I don't want to deal with anything at all. I want infinite rest, permanent rest... no alarm clock, no work, no waking-up-to-go-to-the-bathroom, nothing but oblivion's coital caress.

* * *

I roll over and turn the alarm clock off before it beeps again. It's almost one in the afternoon. I get up and go through my morning ritual, eat a big breakfast, then notice that there's a message on our answering machine.

At first it sounds like a telemarketer... one of those standard Midwasteland accents that could come from nowhere and everywhere. It's a woman's voice.

"We are sorry to inform you that all transaction with your organization have been canceled due to a recent miscommunion of forces. The appropriate parties have been reprimanded. We apologize for any inconvenience you may have experienced in the course of this interaction. As no contracts have been signed, and you have expressly acted through your free will, Holy Writ requires us to inform you that you remain a free and conscious bipedal, three-brained soul-forming agent, able to dwell and develop your soul in relative peace on the planet earth without further demonic possession, infestation, or harassment."

The message stops. There is a choppy break sound, which sounds like a million screams of the damned, like an infinite laugh track over the unfunniest material you've ever seen, *ever*.

A familiar voice goes, "Light-bearer. Forget everything I said. It meant nothing." The message ends. I press the 'save' button to record it, but it doesn't work.

"It meant nothing..." I repeat over to myself. *What does that mean?*

I run myself in mental circles for a short while. I'm not sure whether or not it's just another trick to confuse me or not. It might have been a message from the *eye*. One can never be sure. An eye that never blinks is a terrible thing with which to reckon. It's vaginal and anal and phallic – all at once. And that... is spooky.

Like... *end of the world* spooky.

I'm ready for the day now. I'm ready for *anything*. I don't have to worry anymore about a sudden visit from an imaginary friend, I live with a person whom I love – whom I'm excited to tell I love – and who probably loves me back, and what's more, I'm *jobless*!

But the world's *still* going to end in less than three days.

I grope around for distractions, unable to concentrate, unable to put the pieces together from these dreams, these scrambled visions, the *message from hell* on my answering machine. When the world ends, this will all sort its self out... necessarily.

First I grab a book, but there seems to be no reason to read. We don't own a copy of the Bible, nor would I read it if we had one. If I wanted a laugh I'd turn on the television and get Biblical interpretations from the blue-screen-gold-Bible guy. I have some comic books, but they seem – at this moment – a little silly.

I make myself a mix of vodka, orange juice, and milky-white laxative, sure to settle the bubbly stomach. The drink helps me pass five minutes or so, but it's still almost an hour before Bea comes home.

I rush out of the apartment and get onto a bus. I pay my fare to the smiling teddy-bear-beard bus-driver, then sit down. It's a moment before I realize that I have to wait for almost a *half an hour* before we'll be at the restaurant where Bea works and I can stand up again. This bothers me. I forgot to bring anything to distract myself with.

I decide to stare at all the people, who in turn duck their heads down or look away. It's the middle of the day on a rainy Wednesday, and I fit in traveling alone like most of them, but unlike them I'm anxious and *full* of energy. Nobody else seems too energetic. If only they knew about the upcoming Apocalypse, they'd treat their time differently.

I think again about the dog on the street with the kids and the cops – the wheel just grinds, grinds, grinds on and on.

The tin-can-bus hobbles its way through downtown to the other end of the city. I hop off in a flurry to capture some of my lost momentum. If I hurry I should be able to meet Bea for the end of her shift, at around three.

And yes! I see her. She's standing on the corner outside the restaurant, smoking a cigarette. I slow my walk down when I see somebody standing next to her. It's one of Blake's friends, Alex – this pathetically scrawny candy-cane-boy with too many band patches and buttons on his clothes for his own good. I met him at a party once, when he tried to chat Bea up. He's doing it again, this time with even less tact than before.

I come upon them from behind.

"I heard about your *prick* boyfriend. Blake told me what's been happening. He's off his fucking top... thinks the world's going to end or some shit. You know what people are saying?" He puts a hand in front of Bea and takes her cigarette, not very smoothly.

Bea steps back a little bit, but she still shares the cigarette. "He's not so..."

[T-] 139

It's good that she created that slight distance, because it gives me just enough room to punch Alex in the side of the face so hard that he falls down on the ground.

I hope I broke something. I hope I snapped something in his miserable little weasel-in-to-take-my-girlfriend-sly-fucker psyche.

Overhead from the restaurant's speakers comes some Mexican dance music, heavy with trombones, tubas and the sweet blasts of trumpets. The music accompanies my punch and the blood which streaks from Alex's face onto the pavement.

Cha cha cha.

Bea looks at me. The crowd on the street around us – this district is upscale, but not so much so that people run in terror if a punch is thrown – haven't even reacted yet. Alex is in the middle of getting up, no doubt ready to fight back with all his dinky might, as I say to Bea, "I love you."

"What?" she asks. She blinks, then insists, "Say that *again*."

Cha cha cha.

Alex leans forward and throws a punch at me. I take it in the shoulder, then Bea kicks her leg forward and knees him in the balls. The poor guy crumples over and steps away. For a minute he looks absolutely impish.

"I love you," I repeat.

And I do. And she sees that I do. And she smiles. And she says, "I love you too."

As Alex walks away, he trips, hits the pavement for the third time, this time face first. He does more damage to himself with the trip than Bea and I did to him with the punch and kick.

Tequila!

Bea and I kiss. As we do, I think about how sometimes life's a difficult cross to bear. Most definitely.

This and That
2 Days
1:00 P.M.

"This and That," I say.

[T-] 142

We're in our apartment. We're naked. We talk to one another, play this verbal game, a strange kind of metaphysical, meta-oral love-extension exercise. Words mean so much when you're rushed for time. With all the time in the world, silence seems optimal. When we imagine there's danger – risk of the end, risk of no more words – it's difficult *not* to speak. It's so important for me, when I'm nervous, to talk the time away.

"Me and you," Bea says.

How do we define that division? If she were hurt, wouldn't I feel pain?

She cares for me. I care for her. We're connected.

"God and the Devil," I say.

"Good and Evil," she quickly replies.

"Right and wrong," I chime.

Are these dualities known by one another? Does God understand the Devil, and is it because the Devil thinks he understands God – when, of course, he doesn't – that he is the Devil?

How are we different, with our commercialization of all things, sacred and profane alike? How can people *sell* God? They sure try. And to sell something is to declare mastery over it, isn't it? It's a declaration of ownership.

Nobody owns the ineffable.

What do we know about God, really?

I can just see the big-guy ejaculate, shoot galaxies

from his generative organs outward: a big cosmorgasmic *bang*! It's joyous and terrible – all this creation – because it *one day has to end.* But who's going to use the towel to clean up the whole thing? God or his lover?

Nobody ever mention's God's lover.

Why? God's the divine masturbator, the eternal jerk-off.

"The body and the mind," Bea says.

In my better moments, I think this life is an illusion. In my sublime moments, I *know* it is.

"Hope and fear," I say.

"Love and hate," she says.

"Change and stasis," I say.

Each of these is the absence of the other, in different degrees.

"Rationalism... empiricism," I say, drag the syllables out, one at a time.

Ra-tion-al-ism. Emp-ir-i-cism.

These words hardly mean anything at all, to me, but I use them. You can topple thousands of years of tradition by recognizing the divine paradox of duality, and words deflate in importance very quickly thereafter. Of course, you end up at the beginning, when you question the end. But that's a great place to start, isn't it? I'd suggest the beginning, because starting at the end, like I have tends to drain you of your soul-stuff, of your energy.

"Everything and nothing. White and black. Darkness and light. Up and down. Left and right. Chaos and order. Pleasure and pain. Knowledge and ignorance," I blast out.

"This and that," she adds, nods.

Two days.

Bea patronizes me by playing along with my moods. She thinks this will be over in less than forty-eight hours, and I agree with her but in an entirely different way. She thinks it will be over because absolutely *nothing* will happen, and I'll have to recognize my own temporary insanity, my own fallibility, my humanity. I think it will be over... for the obvious reason.

I haven't told her, and I don't think I will, but I have a few ideas about what could happen:

A. The World ends. Everything ends. Complete annihilation. We've talked about this before, haven't we?

B. I end, but the world keeps going. I don't know why, but maybe the date was meant for me and not the entire world. Maybe I've projected my ego so far outward and this is all a delusion. *Maybe I'm going to die.*

C. Nothing happens. I don't end. The world doesn't end. 6:10 p.m. comes along, becomes 6:11 p.m., and we just go on. All of us live out our lives as we normally would, waiting until 2012 for the next major scare.

I can't imagine that there's a D, all of the above, here... but who knows? Can contradictory events take place in the same moment?

The door snaps open to another dimension.. You look out onto a field of cows, and they have tortured faces. They're staring at you. A Mommy-cow walks up to you and mooooooo's in absolute agony. This time, in this dimension, you aren't so lucky as to be unable to understand cow-talk. You hear every udderance... utterance...

"You ate my baby!"

And you're screaming, backing away from the door as rapidly as you can. A desire to only eat carrots and cabbage overtakes you. You rush into the nearest door to escape the oncoming cows, but you find no rest. Behind this door are thousands, nay, millions of carrots and cabbage...

There is no escape.

It can be a lot like a room full of cows, this übernatural awareness, the *sensitivity* of the damned-fool-martyrs. *You* should know what it's like. I hope you can be honest enough to admit it, or at least be honest enough to hear the words come across and through to you. Honesty is not an internal event. It radiates outward, energizes and reinforces everything that's good and pure. Deceit is completely internal. It withdraws and departs, escapes and creeps. It sucks inward.

Honestly, a creeping part of myself wants to end my life right now, and I would if it weren't for two things: Bea, firstly, and secondly... the anticipation of what's to come. I haven't sweated out these past eight days to not discover what's going to happen.

I would probably jump from a bridge. The moment of flight-emotion before the fall really starts would be the greatest high. I know it would.

Why would I kill myself? Control. It would be nice to feel in control again. But I *am* in control, and I have to remind myself of that.

I think, if there's anything Be'ezlebub said that's worth remembering, it's the stuff about free will. I've always believed in that, and even if suicide might be the only action we can take that's truly free, at least there's a possibility of freedom.

It's not all that dreary, really. The *question* is as complicated as any answer we'll ever have. I think that the answer's a *feeling*, ultimately, and that complicated strings of words betray the effort toward feeling.

You *feel* free or you *feel* bound. Head toward the former feeling, toward that emotional state. It will probably feel warm, and when you find it. Let go of your desire for your control. I'll try and do the same, in the time I have left. This might be worthless, but if B or C happen and not A, then who knows where we'll be in a year?

Old masters would write – perform? I think poetry's always a performance, even when it's written – haiku on their death-beds. Did they do this for posterity or for their own peace of mind?

Probably both.

"Hey, Bea..." We're spacing in and out of speech. I don't know what she thinks about when we sit silently. One of the reasons I love her is because she can sit quietly with me and I with her. This is desirable. *Most* speech is empty noise.

"*I'm not going to.*
Why bother? We'll all be dead.
Anyway, I'm tired."

She laughs a little, a noise like tiny crystals thrown at bells, then says:

"*Not bad, for a guy*
Who's absolutely insane.
I mean... really nuts."

We can't help ourselves. I laugh a little, enjoy the moment enough so that I forget briefly my dread and anxiety. Bea rubs my leg.

t's a clear day out – finally, after two days of heavy rain – and the flood warning has passed. She looks over at me and says, "Life and death?"

"Sure," I reply. I lean back against the couch. "That sounds like as good a distinction as any we've said yet. I don't know why I didn't think about it before." I wiggle my toes a few times, then say, "Today and tomorrow."

The day after *tomorrow...*

Bea sits up and says, "We should go out and do something. I'm sure there's somebody we could call, meet somebody... hang out. I don't know. Anything's better than wasting away in the apartment. You're too *nervous*. You need to get your mind off that all. I can tell."

I shake my head. "This is the only thing I can *have* on my mind right now. What else can I think about? I don't want to put the idea in front of any of our friends. Besides, I sound crazy. I know I sound crazy. I'm miserable company, anyway, without this to plague me. Imagine how I'd be now."

"That's true," she says. "I just thought of another one. Memory and forgetting."

Memory and forgetting.

I think about all the people that I've left and have left me throughout my life. I've rationalized my terrible behavior, intellectualized it, and marginalized it to obscurity. I say things like, "there is an infinite recurrence of polarity." But it just means people grow, people change, some people grow to hate you... some people to love you, some only to *tolerate* you. Friends become enemies become stale memories, onward and onward until it's a bright blaring blur. There are beautiful moments, like this moment now – it's good. I feel okay. I feel *honest*, because I understand finally that I will never understand anything at all.

For a person like me, though, who has never learned how to appreciate other people... what can I expect from social exchange, from where should come the good things in life? The joy of life radiates outward from you. It can't be brought in from the outside. What am I going to do?

There's a bright shining light, or a bright shining eye, on the other side of some chasm, and to cross it people like me have to kill ourselves – not physically, but – morally, mentally, and *spiritually*. We have to take everything we've ever learned and reduce it to *nothing*, then achieve rebirth. It means a complete change of polarity.

If you're one of us and you've figured out how to do this, I feel envious and awed. This is not as easy as it sounds. People who achieve this – whatever it is I'm thinking of. Enlightenment is probably a good word – have a tendencies to laugh and patronize those of us who haven't discovered what they have. They usually speak in strange jargon, in-group-speak, or, worse, in mystical blurbs and snorts. Be careful of the fakers, too. They'll eat you alive, if you invite them in.

They will always ask for money.

And not just a little money. Not money to pay cost. Money to make you broke and powerless. Money to make them rich and sporty.

Some people find a little enlightenment and think it's the whole thing. Then they lose whatever enlightenment they ever had by trying to sell it. This tastes acidic, like thrown-up coffee grinds on a blank canvas which you're forced to lick for a twisted act of performance art.

"X and Z," I say. "That's really what it boils down to. This and that. Us and them. But there's always a synthesis. It's silly to focus on the numerology of the number of days left... those are human denominations..."

Bea cuts me off. "You're like a confused child. You're aware of that, aren't you? I appreciate you, and I appreciate what you are... the potential you have. You have so much, if you could see it and use it. But you're afraid of your *potential*. That's why you have this fantasy about the world ending. You're afraid of your own potential. You know why I think you're afraid?"

"You're giving me a lecture?" I ask.

She ignores my annoyance. "Because you're going to have to get over yourself to be able to use your potential. You're going to have to let yourself come down a little bit... from your delusions. You should listen to yourself sometimes. If you aren't insane – and I don't think you are, really – then what are you? You're *lying* to yourself. Perpetually. So how do I know you aren't lying to me when you say you love me, when you say you care about me... all those things?"

The mood has subtly changed. "Look. I'm *trying* to change, but I can't convince myself of the importance of even getting up in the morning, let alone to stepping out, getting a job... painting. I can motivate myself to take some momentary action, but getting beyond this fear is too much. Just stay with me for another day or two, to see. Tomorrow's Friday, and Saturday's *the* day. I just need to *know* that there's some meaning, before I'm able to start again."

"Even if the world were to end the day after tomorrow, how would that change whether or not there's meaning to the life you've lived already? How would it change whether or not there's meaning to the next few days?"

"It changes everything!" I yell.

I feel like crying.

My teeth grind against one another, my will in tethers. How many times in my life has it been like this, have I felt like this? I want to be in control, but I'm not.

I go on, breathing heavily, "It means there's time to make things different, really different, different for a long time. It means there will be time to make something happen with life, rather than fade away without having achieved anything."

She shakes her head and stands up. "You said the same things a year ago when I met you, and you haven't done much of anything in a *year*. What's one day going to do?" She goes into the bedroom and gets some clothes on. "I want you to come with me, okay?"

I stand and follow her to the bedroom, then get dressed myself. I stumble after her out of your apartment and onto the street outside. She walks ahead of me and in the direction of the E-Z Crunch, my old job, *my old life*. I stop, but she looks back and stares at me then gestures me along with her hand. "You say you love me. Then *trust* me a little."

She looks like an angel, a muse, a higher spirit, the Star of herself. I feel low and moldy, dirty and demonic, confused and cold. I follow. Of course I follow. What else could I do? "I do trust you," I say, like an afterthought, and come to stand at her side.

Outside of the gas station on the corner stands a man with a long wooden staff. The staff leans up against the light post next to him. He's playing a trumpet – not perfectly, but well enough to hold *my* interest. We walk past him on our way into the station, and Bea drops a dollar in the man's case, which prompts an extra flare of blasts from his horn. Bea gives me a strange look, like you would give to a child who's misbehaved.

Is that all I am? A misbehaved child?

We walk into the E-Z Crunch Gas Emporium. I think she wants me to get my old job back.

I'm wrong.

Yes, it's known to happen.

That's not what she wants at all. She avoids the counter and heads toward the bathroom. I follow.

Everything is numb. Being at the old work-place doesn't do much for me. I didn't ever want to see it again.

Luckily, the guy behind the counter is new and doesn't recognize me. He hardly notices our entrance, just chews his bubblegum and reads his magazines. Truly he is one of the proud and the few, select Y's between the X's and the Z's.

What a crunch, this modern way of life... a perpetual fourth quarter hail Mary attempt, down by four points... the whole world, seconds ticking away on the clock, and everybody knows the home team doesn't have a chance.

Bury your head in your towel and pray to Allah, to Christ, to G$d, because you've hedged your bets anyway, and so you'll never really come out a loser. Nobody *loses* anymore. Everybody's a winner, so long as we can convince ourselves of the lies, the lie, the one fundamental dollar sign. Value. We're all valuable. There's *nothing* worthless, anymore. It doesn't matter how debased, how banal, how twisted, or how pathetic. Everything has value. Everybody *must* have value. The alternative – judgement – is too frightening, *requires* too much *responsibility*.

Bea doesn't even acknowledge the unfamiliar attendant but instead walks straight toward the men's bathroom. I wonder what the employee thinks of us as we enter the bathroom together and Bea closes the door behind us. I saw stranger things while working the night shift, cleaned up terrible messes from drunks and... vicious mimes, all those late-night American heartland cum-stained customers.

The last time I was in this bathroom was when I saw the number. The lightbulb was broken and I didn't want to replace it. "Somebody replaced the bulb," I comment beneath my breath after Bea flicks it on.

Bea nods and then shows me the mirror where I saw it, saw the number that changed the past week of my life. On the mirror, faded and smeared from a poor cleaning job, is some writing. It looks like somebody wrote it with lipstick or red marker.

For a Grrrr8 Time, call 2707610.

Bea looks at me. I can't imagine how I look. I squint my eyes, stare a few more seconds, then turn around.

"Do you see that? This is something you created. 27th of July at 6:10. July 27th! Two, seven, zero, seven, six, one, and *zero*! It's lipstick, goddamnit. Somebody scribbled it on the mirror. It's been there for days! Do you see that?" she shrieks. "I came here yesterday before work, just to see. I didn't have the heart to tell you last night, but you should know now. It's just something you made up, all this. Everything about the world ending, your dreams and your visions, everything you've seen and think you've seen – they're all based on this. You don't have to worry anymore!"

I stumble back through the door and rush out the front of the gas station. I trip over a potato chip stand. The chips fly to the ground, but I don't stop. I'm out the front of the station, past the pumps, past a BMW and a man who stares at me like I dropped from the moon. Cars screech to a halt as I stumble across the street, onto the other side of the pavement, and walk everywhere and nowhere all at once.

Shayabellæn
1 Day
Exactly 24 Hours Before the Imminent
Conclusion of All Things

Imagine.

[T-] 158

Could you ever concentrate so hard on one single fact – of if you're not into facts, a single *possible* truth – and make your mind hone in on the divine substrate, the real and true liquid-airy-fiery-essence of all things? If you could do this, would your mind expand or contract? Would a physical sensation accompany the adjustment, or would it be a purely astral or emotional experience? Could you voyage to the starry center and return to talk about it, or would you return older, wiser, but completely dumb, unable to speak, unable to share what you've experienced, with only the wicked knowing look in your eye to say that:

Yes, I've seen the one.

Which one?

The one. Now leave me al-one.

Try it. Report back to me. Better yet – if you get it, I'll know, because your mind will match God's, the fire will meet the water, and we'll all boil over in a wet-sex-slide of joy and cosmic orgasm. The moment - Now - Y - Yes - will repeat infinitely in a loop-tic-twitch, and hopelessness will disappear. Be sure to find something nice to focus on.

Apocalypse is not an easy subject. Even the introductory level course is a killer. Don't take it if you want to maintain a high average. But if you're into risk...

When you become obsessed with an idea like the imminent destruction of everything you've ever known, you start to sweat a little. Your bowel movements become irregular, your mouths goes dry, and wicked visions of little kittens going to early graves – or whatever – fill your in-between-moments.

I didn't go home last night. I wandered around all night in the park. I slept in the pagoda where the jazz band had played that day when I painted. It didn't rain or anything, which is a plus, because my second-to-last night on earth shouldn't be soggy and miserable. Miserable, yes, but I couldn't *stand* soggy.

I feel bad about running away. Bea's probably pissed as hell. I don't know what I'm going to do.

"Do you play chess?" I hear somebody say.

I look down from the steps of the pagoda and over to where an elderly gentleman with a long grey beard sits. His beard is so long it drags almost to his lap. It contrasts surprisingly with his clothing, a flannel shirt and khakis. He sits at a concrete table with a chess board in front of him. I've been so lost in thought I didn't even see him sit down and fold out the chess board. The board is made of green and white cloth, though the pieces are black and white... thick, strong plastic. The pieces look desirable. It would be nice to put one in your mouth.

"Sort of," I reply. I've never been very good at

chess, though I like to play some. My father, who I
don't think about very often, taught me. It makes me
remember, seeing those pieces, the board, this man. "I
don't know that I'm in the mood right now, though."

The old man nods, then gestures to the other
side of the board. He sets up the white pieces on the
empty side. "I usually play with my friend Anton," he
says. He looks over his shoulder, turns back to me.

His friend's dead. I don't have to ask. I just
know. The look in the guy's eyes... the way his voice
trails off. It's sad.

I feel sympathy. It makes no sense. So one
person died, and now this old guy has nobody to play
chess with... how can that matter? But it does. His eyes
are like big blue pools, watery and clear, like the interior
of that vision-pyramid... the eye wide and staring.

One. What can you say about that number?
Infinite subjectivity, infinite objectivity... all things
contained within itself, unaware of anything other than
that-which-it-is. Knowledge of the one is necessarily
knowledge of the self.

If you can discern what you really are, that one
thing beneath all the other layers, then you'll discover
your sublime origins... and your incredible loneliness.
Loneliness doesn't necessarily mean an absence of
company. Loneliness can exist while you're surrounded

by people... but still sense your disconnection. Aware of your *divinity*, you'll feel marginalized by your own understanding of yourself, that thing which nobody else can really ever know.

And this man, with his chess pieces and his park and his watery blue eyes, is all-one. A*lone*. I stand up and move to the other side of the table. The guy doesn't make eye contact with me as I sit down, though he smiles just faintly. He seems startled. He didn't really expect me to sit down.

"Your move," he says quietly. His eyes bore holes of light into the board.

I know before I even make the first move that there's no *way* I'll be this guy, not now, and probably not ever.

I don't care.

These pieces are a pale representation of our intentions. We lay out some rules – an eight by eight board, the six different pieces, castling, et cetera – and we're obliged to obey them for the sake of the game. It's amazing that on such a concrete thing as sixty-four squares so many variations can be created. There is so much room for expression, but always within the container, always within the single, square eye of the mutual vision, the third thing between two players.

If I disagree to how the board works, what will

happen? Will communication crumble, or will I force us to develop a new game? *Do I have to play alone*, if I don't agree with the way you and the rest of the world might play?

Does anyone want to know what happens after the board disappears and we have to start anew, with only our imaginations to carry us off the pathetic concrete table.

I move a pawn.

"I'm sorry about your friend," I say.

Now the guy looks up at me, looks me in the eye, then shrugs. "You don't look too great yourself," he says, comparing me to a corpse.

What the hell, I think. *What can it matter if I tell somebody? He's a complete stranger.* "I think the world's going to end."

The man doesn't so much as hesitate. He scans the board with his eyes, then calmly moves a knight – a "horsey." After the move he says, "I used to think that too, whenever something really terrible happened, I always convinced myself that it was the end of everything." He purses his lips before he adds, "In a way, it always *was*."

See. He doesn't understand me at all. I move a knight. "I don't mean it like that. I mean literally – the world is going to end. I have this... idea... and I can't be rid of it. I *know* the world's going to end."

"When's it supposed to happen?" he asks. He moves a pawn and in so doing threatens one of my pawns.

"Tomorrow," I say. "Twenty four hours from now. Less than that, actually." I move a bishop to reinforce the pawn.

The old man looks at me. "What does your family think about this?" he asks. He enunciates very clearly. He has straight teeth and a strong stare, now that he looks into my eyes.

"I don't really speak to my family."

"That's strange. If the world were to end, I'd want to be with my family and friends. Why are you sleeping in the park?" he asks, honest and open and curious. "Don't you have a girlfriend or something? You look like you should."

"Yeah, but she doesn't understand."

He moves his second knight out from behind his pawns. "That doesn't surprise me."

I lean back from the table, noncommital, not moving. "I don't expect you to understand, either. I just met you."

"So you're saying that the world's going to end – everything, the whole universe – or just the Earth?"

"Everything."

He whistles through his teeth, then snorts out a

laugh, "We're all going to die eventually. Some very smart people have said some very smart things about this throughout the years. What makes you think you'd be the one to know the date? What's your evidence?" He pauses, looks at the board, "It's your move."

I lean my hand forward and castle without thinking. "I don't need a lecture. It's this feeling I have. I can't explain it... not succinctly. It's like all the desperation and anxiety crawled onto my back – like some deranged chimp – to claw at my head. I recognize the incredible nature of the notion, and I accept that it's delusional, but I can't shake the *feeling*."

"You should eat more fruit," the old man mutters. I squint my eyes, annoyed, and he notices it. "Look," he says. "We're all going to die sometime. The universe *doesn't just end*. I don't think people become *less* when they die. I think we become *more*. So maybe your revelation is something like that – maybe you're just misinterpreting the signs."

"You have a lot to say for a complete stranger."

"I'm not a complete stranger. I'm half way to beating you at a game of chess," he says, a smile on his face. His voice his high and clear. He enunciates perfectly. He moves a bishop.

"I met somebody a few days ago who said a lot of the same things, about misinterpretation... and he wasn't somebody I'd really ever put much trust in."

"It's your choice, young man."

I laugh, laugh, laugh – upward, stare at the blue sky laughter. "Yeah," I say. "I know it's my choice." I finger the edges of the board. "Don't let me make you worry," I say. I hardly look at the pieces before I move a knight.

"You aren't making me worry. Even if the world ended, I wouldn't mind. What could I do? The more years you live the more people come and go from your life, the more times you come and go from the lives of others, the more you begin to see that people are like planets, like wandering stars. We have satellites – some of us – and sometimes those satellites get bumped into orbit. Sometimes people are like stars... big glowing, bright things. Some people are like black holes, always taking."

He pauses in his speech, shrugs... then goes onward like it's an everyday thing, "Maybe you and your girlfriend are a binary star system. Or maybe she's just a moon, and you're waiting for some larger body to bump her out of orbit. I don't know. It's your thing, isn't it?"

"That's not true. We're connected."

"It's a strange thing then, to sleep in a park when you have another place to be. You should be back there with her. If the world's really going to end, then that's where you should be – family. If she's what matters, then doesn't that make sense?" The game is put on hold. "Why did you leave in the first place?"

"I... she's passed this off as something psychological. This past week has been vicious – I've seen things..."

"I've heard that before. How much did you take?"

"Nothing!" I shout. "Honestly... I've just seen things, dreams and visions and things. I know what you're thinking about, and I've been sober for over a week. I don't know that I'll ever touch another hallucinogen..."

"Okay," the old man says. He puts his arms upon the table. "Just... think about this. Even if the world's going to end tomorrow, even if you, your girlfriend, me, this chess board... everything is going to cease to be... what good is worrying about? Will you be able to stop the end from coming?"

That's a good point.

"That's... a good point," I admit, remembering to say what I think.

"At any given moment, in any given day, at any given place... you'll never know. There's always risk. There's no point *not* living. *That's* death." He leans back from the table. "I tell you what. You need to get home to your friend. She's probably worried about you. Let's stop this game here and pick up where we left off. I have a good memory, and we've only made a few moves."

"Sure," I say. I feel slightly better. I feel almost excited. I have something to look forward toward.

"I'll see you here tomorrow night, barring apocalypse?"

I nod and stand. I extend my hand, and he extends his. We shake. "What's your name?" I ask him.

"John," he replies. He looks up at me, smiles. "I'll see you tomorrow, friend."

He doesn't ask my name, and I don't give it to him. I will, if the world doesn't end.

And what would I have told him if he had asked? Does my given name represent me? I feel changed. It's new. Everything's new. I'm new. And the end is nigh.

"If the universe was created, it can be undone," John says as I walk away, "but as long as there is one good thing left... it won't happen. The universe exists to perpetuate the good, to make good possible. We're all small versions of the universe, anyway. So what's that tell you?"

Ten yards or so away from the table, I turn around... I almost expect to see that John's really Be'ezlebub, and this is some sort of trick. I see what I should have expected to see: an old man in front of a chess board, delicately packing his pieces away...

[T-] 168

probably excited for his next game with a new, albeit insane, friend.

I walk toward home. It's still light outside, still before eight o'clock. It's a bright day, perfect for a swim. As I'm walking, I hear something that catches my attention. Somebody's playing a trumpet. It sounds like it comes from above me. I look around, but there are only houses. I head toward the sound, which leads me into a driveway. When I come around the driveway and look up, there's a small deck attached to a back room of a weird-looking blue house. The house is too tall. It looks as if it was cut in half down the middle from the top to the bottom.

The two brothers from the coffee house are there. One of them, the younger one, is responsible for the trumpet playing. The other one reads over the blasting of the trumpet: "Suddenly a red Dragon appeared, with seven heads and ten horns, and seven crowns on his heads. His tail drew along behind him a third of the stars, which he plunged to the earth. He stood before the woman as she was about to give birth to her child, ready to eat the baby as soon as it was born."

The other brother stops playing his trumpet. "Wild," he says, laughing. "Who would eat a bay-bay?"

The older brother smiles, then continues, "She gave birth to a boy who was to rule all nations with a

[T-] 169

heavy hand, and he was caught up to God and to his throne. The woman fled into the wilderness, where God had prepared a place for her, to take care of her for 1,260 days."

"Why that number of days?" the younger one asks.

"I don't know. 28 divides into it 45 times. It could be symbolic. It's roughly three and a half years. It's *probably* symbolic of something, maybe an event that's supposed to happen, maybe an event that happened, maybe an event that never has, never will happen. I don't know. Maybe it's related to the stars."

"Sounds like a load of crap to me," the younger one says, then happily blasts his horn. The older one smiles, then glances down over the side of the deck. He looks at me long and hard, no doubt wondering what the hell I'm doing in their driveway. I lift my hand a wave a bit, and he returns the wave silently. I step back from where I came and head back home.

No matter what happens, I'm going to record the clock - ticking - anxious - memory - moments... those final blasts of time. I have a clock and a stop watch set perfectly to the time.

Bea left a note on the kitchen table.

I don't understand why you left. It's just

further evidence that you can't deal with life. We need to talk, not run away from one another. That's the last time you'll ever run away from me, got it? I'm out, and I'm not sure when I'll come back.

I feel ill. I don't know whether I'm coming down with something, or whether or not it's just you that I'm sick of. How can you say that you love me, then run away when I show you something as simple as the truth? If I'm not home by 6:10, you'll have to deal with the Apocalypse on your own. Otherwise, I'll call you at 6:15 and we can laugh about your stupidity.

- Beatrice

That's my girl.

A few hours pass in dreaded silence. It's almost midnight. I'm looking at the painting I made. It's distracting, to look over something you created. It's so easy to be critical of yourself, so easy to analyze until you lose the meaning, if there ever was one in the first place.

I read these pages, these things I've written, and

I smile, laugh, wonder at myself.

No matter what happens, if 6:10 comes and goes, and the world remains the same, I won't write another line in this. I won't have anything else to say. If I have to go on with life – if some cosmic force doesn't reverse all activity and create... nothing – if Armageddon doesn't come, my life is going to be a lot more interesting than it ever was before.

I feel nervous. I go to the bathroom and take a few sleeping pills. I want to reach the unexpected as quickly as possible so that this nerve-wracking nervousness passes before I lose it completely. I yearn for the end of this confusion.

I feel like I did when I was a kid the day before Christmas, those long hours before you open your presents... the meal, and of course the dishes have to be done before the family can sit down around the tree. Those are magic moments, moments that form you... high-energy, higher-octave moments. If, in your waking memory, they outweigh the negative, crippling moments, maybe you'll find heaven when you die, maybe *before* you die. Your angels will lift you up – not in some distant future, but *now*, today – and blow their horns, bring you to the Kingdom and the Glory Now and Forever. You do this. Your angels are you. Your demons are you.

[T-]172

You *are* potential.

* * *

I fall asleep, a deep, beautiful, pill-induced coma that lasts through the night. I wake up and pace around the apartment. The last day is grey, overcast, but with a threatening glare... the sun screams to come out, and it gets close a few times but doesn't succeed.

I have no more visions to share. I spend the day sitting silently. I meditate on nothing until six o'clock comes around. I don't eat. I hardly drink. I hardly *blink*.

Waves of panic shimmer like the heat in a dessert. Our air-conditioned doesn't work, and we are out of water. This highway is growing very short, and the car is becoming cramped.

Waves of terrible panic, fear, raw and unchecked, sweep over me. I can hear words in my head, and they aren't my own. I look at the clock every minute... every second.

The alarm reads **6:00** p.m.
The alarm reads **6:01** p.m.
I take a drink of water.
The alarm reads **6:02** p.m.
I go to the mirror.
I have four faces. I look at myself with my chin

[T-]173

in the air. I look at myself with my head tilted down. Demonic. Be'ezlebub. I look at myself from the left, from the right... pouting, smiling, laughing, crying, hoping, fearing, wanting, taking, having, neeeeeeeeding.

"You have four faces. You never show them."

Yesterday, today, tomorrow... all these things come up again, threaten to overtake me. I feel dizzy. Is this possible, that we've come this far? I'm typing as the moments tick away. I'm here, writing this, in these moments... typing the time away.

The phone rings.

I look at my stopwatch.

6:08:32 p.m., seconds and counting.

The phone rings again.

6:08:40 p.m.

Panic, miserable wicked panic, and I'm inside of it. A bubble of air encloses me, and I see the way that I see. Inside my mind there is a universe, an entirety of understanding. If I tap into that wholly, I'll see more than I could ever hope to understand. When I prick the surface, I see things, hear voices, and I confuse myself. I'm meant to. I'm a lightbearer. I'm supposed to go into those depths. That's what I do, whether or not I'd like. It's where I am as much as what I am.

Who else can I hold the light for?

[T-]174

I should be asking myself this every day. I should have asked myself this long ago.

The phone rings again. It rings a fourth time. I'm frozen in panic. I don't want to talk to anybody. I can't. I have to write. I have to stay close to this source, this glowing light here, the ideas, alive and real.

The answering machine picks up.

Hello! We're not here right now, so leave a message... if it's really all that important.

Our voices together, a weird mix. Low and high. It's strange to hear my voice – unreal.

"Are you there? I know you're there," Beatrice says. There's a pause, a fuzzy crackle on the machine. "I'm sorry I'm not home right now. I don' t know I don't know I don't know! I have something to tell you. Are you there?" She sounds worse than I feel.

I'm frozen where I stand. Frozen inside. I swear my heart skips a beat. Another beat. Is it ever going to start beating again? Am I already dead? Has it ended already? Everything?

No. The clock's moving. I can't be dead. How long can I hold my breath? How long can I stay disconnected? How many seconds have passed?

6:09:04

Anxious, rumbling words, they rumble. I know what she's going to say before she says it, but the words are *still* important. The tone is important. The depth is inescapable, immense, serious beyond serious.

"I'm coming home," she says. "I was just at the doctor. I need to tell you something. It's really important. I hope you're okay. Pick up if you're there."

6:09:14

"Pick up!" she yells.

I dart over to the phone and pick it up. The answering machine beeps.

"Bea," I say. "I'm here."

"I was worried about you," she says. "Where were you last night!?"

I look at my watch. **6:09:30**

"I... I couldn't come home. Are you okay? Why were you at the doctor?"

"You know how I've been sick lately?" she says, a statement and a question and an exclamation all at once.

"Yeah," I respond. Sweat drips off my face and onto the phone, little rolling beads of fluid slip and slide and do the liquid shuffle down the smooth, smooth plastic. "What is it? You don't have anything serious...?"

6:09:40

"No. It's not like that."

"Bea, I think it's about to happen," I say. "It's over."

6:09:50

"No, it's not! You're paranoid. This is more important. I have to tell you this *right now*. Forget about all that crap. We have to make a decision. This is really important!"

6:09:55

I say nothing.

6:09:56

I don't know what to say. My mind is void. *I* am void. If there was ever anything inside me, it's gone. I'm gone, blown away, the pyramid pulled from its roots to reveal something far more perfect, a system far older than anything I or you or we could ever devise.

6:09:57

"I'm pregnant."

6:09:58

A simple declaration. A miracle of forces. All things come to bear.

Out of the corner of my eye a ray of sunlight creeps through the clouds, blasts through our curtains, and presses fiercely against the sheets of our bed.

I open my mouth...

exhale...

Epilogue:

"Of him who found out all things, I shall tell the land,
Of him who experienced everything, I shall tell teach the
whole.
He searched the lands, everywhere.
He who experienced the whole gained complete wisdom.
He found out what was secret and uncovered what was hidden,
He brought back a tale of times before the Flood.
He had journeyed far and wide, weary and at last resigned.
He engraved all toils on a memorial monument of stone."

The Epic of Gilgamesh
Myths from Mesopotamia, Oxford

Kevin Anthony Kautzman
is not an authority on *the* Apocalypse – only apocalypse.
He studies philosophy, history, and Aikido, and is into
well-lighted rooms.
More information can be gleaned about Kevin and **[T-]** –
as a spoken word project, and as revelation – at
www.cassielalpha.com.